DON'T TEMPT ME

Also by Ziggy Harris

Not In His Shadow

DON'T TEMPT ME

A novel by
Ziggy Harris

This book is a work of fiction. Names, characters, places, and incidents are the product of the author's imagination or are used factiously, and any resemblance to actual persons living or dead, business establishments, events, or locales, is entirely coincidental.

This book is dedicated to readers who love love.

To my friends and family who have supported me and my art through the years, thank you! To the readers and supporters across the globe, thank you! I am forever grateful for the time you spend with me and the journey you take when reading about the lives of dynamic characters. Characters I hope resonate with you and that you see yourself in.
Enjoy ★

Don't Tempt Me

Bailey

In college Bailey was head over heels for the San Diego Oilers defensive lineman Casey Christopher. He has built like a God; his sculpted body made men envious and left women yearning. Casey's body was tatted like a New York City subway station. He was covered from head to toe with well over 40 pieces of art across his body except his unmentionables, hands, face, and feet. She did not typically go for guys with locs, but because he kept his neat and clean, Bailey wanted to lay on his chest and play in them. Casey also had the most kissable lips she had ever seen on a man. She had the blues for the bad boy of the American Football League, but as the new public relations intern for the Oilers, she learned she would need to keep her left shoulder devil at bay.

****

Bailey Jones relocated from Los Angeles to San Diego to take a public relations internship with the San Diego Oilers. During the first semester of her senior year of

1

college, Bailey wowed the Oiler's recruiters at the Los Angeles State University job fair in the fall of 2011. As a Communications major at LASU, Bailey concentrated on public relations; she enjoyed the fast-paced environment and shaping public perceptions. She felt empowered to influence the public's perception of an individual, group, or company.

During her junior year at LASU, Bailey interned for The Beat, an online magazine, as an assistant to the editor-in-chief, Sharla Campbell. Sharla was a hard-nosed investigative reporter committed to releasing accurate celebrity news. She was not concerned about gossip or hearsay; Sharla had learned in Los Angeles people would say or do anything to plant a story for fifteen minutes in the limelight. She loathed attention whores and upheld the integrity of The Beat by holding her contributors to the highest investigative regard. Each story went to print once it was cross-referenced at least twice.

Bailey learned a lot from Sharla while interning at The Beat. The most important thing she learned as a professional in a dog-eat-dog world was all she had was her word, integrity, and never to compromise them. Now, as an intern for the American Football League, she knew it was critical now more than ever not to compromise her reputation, regardless of any potential gains. As if concerning herself with the global image of one of the AFL's top teams, Bailey had to learn how to navigate foreign territory; working with professional athletes and their "handlers," as she liked to refer to agents, managers, and entourages. As a public relations intern, Bailey worked with the Oilers Foundation to plan community events for various charitable causes with an array of audiences, corporate to communities in need, and everything in between.

****

Bailey greeted the receptionist sitting at the large desk on the open ground floor of the Oilers corporate offices and training facility in Mission Valley, north of San Diego's city center. The older woman had been with the organization for well over thirty years. "Good morning, Sally!" Bailey said to a red-haired woman.

"Good morning, Bailey! How was your weekend?" Sally asked.

"My weekend was great. I have been preparing for my first day of work. I can't believe how nervous I am," replied Bailey, "How was your weekend?" she asked.

Sally was the first person to show any sign of being human to Bailey when she arrived at Oilers Central for her second interview. Bailey placed Sally to be in her late fifties or early sixties, who was full of life as she always greeted everyone who walked through the doors of Oilers Central with a smile. Bailey was relieved by the older woman's sweet disposition because her boss, Jonathan Starks, was as lovely as a porcupine.

"It was wonderful; Jim and I took the grandkids to the beach. We are trying to enjoy the great outdoors before it becomes too hot." Sally gushed.

"I definitely understand," Bailey responded, "This SoCal heat is brutal. Well, Sally, I better get going, I do not want to be late on my first official day of work."

Beaming at the young woman before her, Sally responded, "Okay, dear, I'll catch you later."

Don't Tempt Me

Bailey

Bailey had been working tirelessly for two solid weeks on SummerFest, which was scheduled for the weekend following the July 4th holiday. SummerFest was the annual event hosted by the Oilers where local youth community football teams would get a chance to tour At Comm Stadium, play flag football, learn football drills, and talk to the pros about what it takes to make it to the American Football League. Much to Bailey's surprise, when she started working for the Oilers, she found that the planning for SummerFest had yet to begin and was scheduled for just over a month away.

Silently cursing John, Bailey was upset that no one had started working on the event before her arrival. It was well past 6 pm on a Friday, and Bailey wanted nothing more than to go to her apartment and soak in some vitamin D while the sun was still up. With her luck, she would be satisfied with leaving the building before 8pm.

Having made significant gains with an event of this magnitude in three weeks, the last items on Bailey's agenda were to send invitations, arrange transportation for participating programs, and to get as many players as possible to commit to the festivities. It was common for lesser-paid players or players in contract negotiations to forego these kinds of events. However, with training camp in full swing, Bailey hoped to persuade more players to volunteer their time with the activities instead of relying on external volunteers.

Bailey knew that players were unwilling to commit to community events if it was not a contractual obligation, and she could not blame them. Football was a tricky business, with contracts not being guaranteed and pushing their body to extreme limits; she could not blame those players who wished not to participate. Still, she kept hope alive. Bailey was putting the finishing touches on her compelling presentation that she hoped would encourage the team to join SummerFest.

****

Grabbing her purse from the bottom left drawer in her cubicle desk, Bailey gathered her pink blazer, that she had worn with a denim pencil dress, from the back of her desk chair. As she prepared to exit the building and head for the employee parking lot, Bailey made a pit stop at the ladies' restroom located a few feet away from the exit on the ground floor of Oiler's Central. Startled by what she'd seen as she entered the bathroom, Bailey quickly turned around to exit. "Hey!" The voice called out. Bailey did not respond as she kept walking. "Hey, miss, could you please stop?" Slowing her stride, Bailey turned to see what the person wanted. "I apologize if I alarmed you," he said, "but the men's room is being cleaned, and I could not wait. I didn't know there was anyone left in the building."

Bailey's eyes ascended from the floor until she looked into the eyes of Casey Christopher, defensive tackle for the Oilers. "It's okay, I totally understand," was all Bailey could muster. Bailey's mind wondered as Casey stood before her, wearing black and grey gym shorts, a black tank top and black and red Air Jordan retro six sneakers. Bailey tried to calm her nerves, but the print in his gym shorts made it hard for her to focus.

"Are you sure?" he broke into her reverie.

"Uh-umm, yes, I thought I had to go to the bathroom, but it turns out that I don't have to", she responded.

Rocking back on his heels, Casey countered, "The way you bum rushed the bathroom door, I would have thought otherwise," before chuckling. Bailey was doing her best to remain calm, and she could not decipher if he were mocking her or being genuine. The added nervousness and staring at one of her many crushes in the eyes added to Bailey's growing urge to relieve herself.

"Well," she began, "Mr. Christopher, you would be correct. If you do not mind, I would like to use the restroom now." Feigning confidence while walking past the bank of sinks, Bailey scrambled to the nearest stall when she heard the door of the bathroom close behind her. After relieving herself, Bailey readjusted her clothes and added a fresh coat of lip gloss. "Shit!" Bailey cursed under her breath as she exited the restroom.

"What did I do now?" Casey asked as he stood near the exit door of Oilers Central.

"Why are you still here?" Bailey asked with an ounce of bite and apprehension.

"You didn't expect for me, a gentleman, to leave you in this here deserted building all alone, did you?" Casey answered.

"That would have been preferred," Bailey responded as she rolled her eyes.

"Clearly, little lady, you have no idea of who I am. Plus, my father would kill me," Casey said as he opened the exit door for Bailey to exit, "Now, where did you park?"

"You can't be serious; I can make it to my car from here, thanks, though," Bailey responded.

Casey said nothing. His eyes grew serious as his jaw clenched. Bailey could not pinpoint what she saw in Casey's eyes, but from what she gathered, he was a man who did not take to being challenged. On either account, Bailey decided that his kind gesture would not be one she would quarrel over. Instead, she pointed to the right of the building and said, "This way."

Bailey and Casey walked in an awkward silence until they reached her lipstick-red Charger. "Well, this is me," Bailey said matter-of-factly to Casey.

"Is that right?" Casey followed in disbelief at the vehicle the little lady drove, "This looks like the ride of a dope boy. You sure this is your whip?"

"Ha-ha, hilarious," Bailey countered, "This was a graduation present from my father; before you ask, no, he is not a d-boy."

"Pops must be a baller," Casey commented as he opened the driver's door of the tricked-out car equipped with a custom interior, tinted windows, and custom rims. Casey held the door open as he watched Bailey make herself comfortable in the driver's seat. When Casey closed her car door, Bailey let down the window to express her gratitude. "Thank you, Mr. Christopher. I appreciate your chivalry."

"Please, call me Casey. Mr. Christopher makes me sound old."

"Well, then, Casey, thank you for your superior concierge service and seeing me to my car."

Casey watched as Bailey maneuvered the vehicle from its parking spot in the employee lot. "It was my pleasure," Casey muttered as he watched the red car with a vanity license plate that read "LADYBUG" drive out of sight.

Casey

"Bro, you should have seen her face when she saw me in the women's bathroom!" Casey said in between sets of bicep curls. "She looked mortified, and all I was doing was washing my hands," he added with a laugh.

"But is she fine?" Jamal asked.

Jamal Scott was the right guard for the San Diego Oilers. A native of San Diego, Jamal was drafted in the third round the same year as Casey out of the University of San Diego. It was rare for linemen on opposite sides of the ball to build solid friendships. Casey and Jamal were different, they were more than teammates, they were brothers. Though highly competitive, they used that energy as motivation to improve their individual skills and abilities. In the last four seasons, they bet on which team, offense or defense, would have the better season: points earned versus points allowed.

Casey was like a lost puppy when he arrived in San Diego for organized team activities; much to his delight, Jamal's family adopted him. Casey loved the Scott family dearly, and having a family he could rely on when his own was thousands of miles away made life, especially the holidays, more tolerable. "I can't lie, shorty was fine." Casey bragged as he dapped up his compadre.

"Well, hook a brother up then." Jamal pleaded, "You know a smooth, handsome fella, such as myself knows how to treat a lady."

"Yeah, not going to happen. She'll send you to the hills quicker than you could get off the line of scrimmage," Casey countered. He hoped his friend did not detect the protectiveness in his voice as he spoke about Bailey.

"Aww man, why are you blocking?" Jamal asked, feigning hurt and disappointment.

Starting a new set of bicep curls, "Not blocking, just trying to warn you. Honey, damn near had me shaking in my J's for wanting to walk her to her car," Casey replied.

Convinced his friend was sweet on the lady they discussed, "Just remember, you do have a family." Jamal's words pierced Casey; he loved his son, but the relationship with his son's mother was beginning to weigh on him.

"Please do not bring Monica up; I'm trying to have a pleasant workout," Casey grumbled.

"No problem slick, I won't say another word."

****

"Fellas, before we get started, someone from upstairs wants to talk to you about an upcoming event", Coach Harold Melvin informed the room full of men dressed in various athletic wear. A collective moan came over the room from the men as their head coach left the lectern.

Dressed in red wide leg pants and a cream printed chiffon collar shirt, an extremely nervous Bailey walked down the center aisle. Praying not to stumble in her nude Christian Louboutin platform heels Bailey approached the front of the room. Preparing to take on some of the world's most physically intimidating men she mentally rehearsed her pitch. Taking her place at the lectern, Bailey heard the loud music of a phone notifying its owner of an incoming call or text message. Centering herself, Bailey began to speak to the room of warriors.

****

"That's her," Casey texted Jamal as he watched the beautiful and confident woman stroll past the eyes of admirers. Casey thought he had seen the woman give him a light smile. Unsure if the gesture was natural or imagined, he decided to believe she could recognize him in a room full of amazons. If you had asked Casey five minutes ago, he would have told you that he could not care less what the people upstairs had to say. Now that this angel was standing before him, he was all ears and eyes.

"So, as you see," Bailey began, "we are mindful of your contractual obligations. However, we want to provide the youth of San Diego a unique experience. One only you can give them. Your expertise could potentially change the trajectory of these boys' lives." Bailey had used every trick in the book to pull on these giant's heartstrings. Some were from troubled upbringings, while others had children themselves. No matter their current or past circumstance, Bailey presented a scenario that would cause them to consider participating in the upcoming SummerFest.

Casey watched as Bailey left the dais to hand out packets to each row for players to review the material for the upcoming event. Casey's contract required him to participate in at least four foundation events, and the annual SummerFest was his favorite. However, with the lady he admired leading the campaign, he volunteered for a leadership role to spend more time with her.

Bailey

Bailey had been working like a mad woman after she met with the players that morning, and it continued well into the afternoon. Startled by the shrill of her office phone, Bailey quickly swung her desk chair around to oblige the demand for the small piece of office equipment. "This is Bailey," she answered on the phone.

"You have a call," the receptionist, Geneva, said as she transferred the call, not waiting for Bailey's response. Bailey waited for the double beep, which indicated a successful call transfer, "This is Bailey," she said for a second time.

"Bailey!" The pleasant yet unfamiliar voice said on the opposite end of the line, "Hi, how are you?"

"I'm sorry, who might this be?" Bailey asked of the gentlemen who had contacted her.

"This is Casey. Don't tell me that you have forgotten about me already", he feigned being hurt by her not recognizing him.

Rising in her seat, Bailey scrambled to locate her notes for the SummerFest, "Uh, Casey, no, I have not forgotten you. I just did not recognize your voice."

Hearing the rustling of papers in the background, "Did I catch you a bad time?" Casey asked.

"Oh, no, what can I help you with?" Bailey asked, hoping that he was calling to discuss the SummerFest.

"SummerFest, and the real question is what can I do to help you? Did you know that it is one of my favorite events?" Casey inquired.

"No, I did not know that this was one of your favorites and thank you for volunteering. You are the first player to reach out. I surely hope more of you guys feel compelled to help", Bailey admitted. "Is there something in particular you would like do at SummerFest?"

"I did have an idea or two that I would like to share with you, but I would like to discuss them in person," Casey replied.

"Sure! No problem," Bailey started. "I am working on the logistics for SummerFest right now, but I can take a break from that for a while. I can see if there is an open

conference room available. What time can you be up here?
Bailey asked.

"No!" Casey cursed himself, and his response was sharper than he intended it to be. Clearing his throat, he followed, "I mean, I have a few things that I'm about to do, and I do not feel like heading back to OC." Taking a deep breath, Casey continued, "Would it be possible for us to meet somewhere?" There was a long pause, and Casey checked his phone to see if the call had been disconnected.

Bailey felt uneasy at Mr. Christopher's request, "If it is better for you, we can meet tomorrow…"

Casey did not want to lose his opportunity, "I really have these great ideas, and I have to get them out before I forget them," for dramatic effect, he added, "You know us football players aren't good with memory. Hazards of the job."

Bailey felt conflicted. Was it appropriate to meet with a player outside of the office, even if it was to discuss Oilers' business? "Hmmm, sure, we can meet this evening." Against her better judgment, Bailey continued, "Does 6 pm work for you?"

Fist pumping for his victory, "The earliest that I could make is 6:30 pm, and that's if we meet downtown." Casey replied, "You know traffic can be crazy."

"Okay, 6:30pm," Bailey begrudgingly responded. "What is your number? So, I can text you for the exact meeting location."

****

Bailey arrived at Casa la Vida fifteen minutes late; she scanned the restaurant looking for the man she had dinner plans with. "Where could he be?" Bailey asked herself. Instead of standing at the restaurant's entryway, Bailey strolled around the restaurant, hoping to locate her dinner companion. As she made her way past the bar, Bailey noticed that there was an alcove off to the left; as she crooked her neck to get a better view, she saw the profile of a very handsome man. Making her way to the secluded section of the restaurant, Bailey gathered her thoughts. She vowed to keep it strictly professional with Mr. Christopher despite feeling like a giggly schoolgirl whenever she was in his presence. Little did Casey know

Bailey had a crush on him in college, and now that she was a professional working for the Oilers said crush was now unacceptable and inappropriate. Never did Bailey imagine that she would be working for the Oilers, and as the universe would have it, low and behold, there she was, working for the Oilers and preparing to have a dinner meeting with the bad boy of the American Football League, Casey Christopher.

Making her final strides to the table, Bailey took a deep breath, "Casey, hey, my apologies for being late." Bailey was awestruck when Casey stood in her presence and hugged her for a greeting.

"It's cool, any longer and I would have thought that you stood me up," he teased.

"Oh no, I would not do that," Bailey reassured him. "In this industry one only has their word and integrity." Placing her sweater on the back of the chair, Bailey continued, "Plus, you are doing me a favor by contributing to the SummerFest. I would not pass up any opportunity to discuss it."

Bailey and Casey discussed SummerFest and Casey's increased leadership role and responsibilities for hours. She found it surprisingly easy to talk to Casey; in addition, Bailey found his perspective to be refreshing. At a quarter after ten, Bailey excused herself and thanked Casey for stepping up with SummerFest and covering the cost of her meal. The two debated on who would cover the dinner bill while waiting for it to arrive, and it turned out Bailey was slow to check. Bailey had plead her case to cover the bill, and when that plea had fallen on deaf ears, she insisted on paying her portion. Much to her dismay, Casey did not allow that either. Bailey felt a sense of triumph when she coaxed Casey into letting her cover the tip. Though he had already added the tip when he paid, he did not battle too much with Bailey when she insisted on leaving the tip.

****

"Mina, answer the phone," Bailey said hurriedly, drumming her fingers on her car's steering wheel. Bailey was at a red light, hoping her best friend would pick up. "Mina?" Bailey asked on the third ring, hoping she heard the phone being answered.

"Yeah, what's up?" The sleepy voice on the other end of the line responded.

"Did I wake you? I am so sorry; I need someone to talk to," Bailey pled, hoping that her friend did not have to be at work too early the next day.

"Naw, girl you good. I was on set for thirty hours straight, yesterday, and today. The good thing is, I do not have to return until three tomorrow afternoon, so you're good. What's up?"

Bailey and Mina had been friends since junior high school. They met in seventh grade at Drew Middle School in San Francisco. Mina was a transfer student from Texas and found Bailey friendly compared to the other girls in her classes. Mina's father was in the military and had recently retired before moving his family west to be near Mina's mother's family. A natural athlete, Mina ran cross country and track for Drew. Drew was known for its academic excellence and superior athletics department. Unfortunately, Drew lacked one thing Mina missed about Texas: Black people. The number of Black students, teachers, and staff was minimal.

"I had dinner with Casey Christopher tonight." Bailey blurted out.

"You did what?" Mina was aghast.

"Well, it was for the SummerFest. You know that big event I told you about?" Bailey explained, "Well it turned out that he had some ideas on how to get more players involved."

"So, what's the big deal," Mina asked.

Considering her words wisely, "I think I like him," Bailey admitted.

"Bails," Mina sounded exhausted, "do you want to go down that road with a professional athlete? You see all that Nyh has gone through with Julius, and they started dating in high school."

Bailey was silent for a long while as she pondered her friend's response. It was no secret that their friend Nyhrie got played by her basketball superstar boyfriend, now husband. Did Bailey want the distraction of being romantically involved with a professional athlete? Could she handle the consequences of such a relationship?

"You know Mina," Bailey started, "you're right. I think I was overcome with excitement. You know I have had a crush on Casey for years. It is not every day a girl can work with her crush. Especially when he is a superstar."

Ziggy Harris

Casey

"Monica, I am tired of playing these games with you!" Casey shouted to his girlfriend. "You act so childish and play too many games. Are you with me for me? Or are you with me for the money?"

"Really? Casey?" An affronted Monica responded. "Do you really think I am with you for the money? I cannot believe you! How about, I'm with you because I love you. Or, because we have a son together? Do not insult me and diminish our relationship to be about money!" Monica shouted as she stormed out of their bedroom.

Making his way to Josiah's room, Casey checked on the sleeping toddler. The last five years of Casey and Monica's relationship had been stressful. Casey loved JoJo; he would go to the end of the earth and back for that boy, but Casey knew he was not ready for children. Casey assumed that Monica had been on birth control. They had been together, on and off, for four years before she got pregnant. Monica was not the same woman he met when they were in college since he had been drafted. To him, she had become complacent with life and more consumed with the glamorous life and being a cliché baller's girl.

****

Monica and Casey met in their sophomore year at Louisiana University in Baton Rouge, Louisiana. Casey could still remember the day he met Ms. Green. It was the first day of the fall semester in Dr. Johnson's English class. Casey ran late because he overslept after his morning football strength and conditioning session. When Casey arrived to the crowded lecture hall, the only vacant seat he could identify was in the middle of the second row. Positioned between a chubby guy and a sweet-smelling young woman. Casey looked to his left and smiled at her as he adjusted himself in the seat. After class, Casey finessed his way into a conversation with the young woman by asking what he missed in the first half of the class. For several weeks after, Casey purposefully went to class late enough to find a seat near his crush, next to or behind her; Casey wanted to be near Monica.

Casey's efforts would soon pay off as one fateful October morning, the woman he admired would acknowledge his existence. "Why are you *always* sitting by me? You like me or something?" The fast-talking woman confidently asked.

Caught off guard by her accusation, Casey grabbed the back of his neck to alleviate his anxiety. "I do," he said with as much confidence as a choir boy. "In fact," he continued, "I would like to take you on a date." From that moment on, Casey and Monica were inseparable. When Casey was drafted right before graduation in her senior year, Monica took a leap of faith and followed Casey to San Diego despite her original plan of returning to New York for law school.

****

Casey drove for hours to clear his head and to make sense of his life. While he could not solve all his problems, he was able to come to one conclusion: he would need to end his relationship with Monica. After nine years, he knew he could never share his heart again with the woman he had a child with. Casey admonished himself for becoming comfortable in their arrangements. Monica made his life easier- sometimes, but Casey knew he wanted and needed something more than someone who kept house. Curse him for not requiring Monica to pursue her own goals. Though moving to San Diego was Monica's idea, Casey was glad she made that decision because he had been so lonely in San Diego. Now, he was not sure if that was a good idea.

Bailey

Bailey was knee-deep in planning the final touches for SummerFest when her office phone rang. Much to her surprise, Casey said, "I have another idea," he said when Bailey answered the phone. Casey no longer needed to be connected to Bailey by the receptionist, as she had given him her direct office number.

"Great! What is it?" Bailey asked. Casey could not detect if Bailey was genuinely excited or stifling annoyance by his call. To keep his spirits up, Casey believed the former was true.

"Not over the phone," Casey started, "Let's talk about it over lunch".

"Casey?"

"I am heading to Il Fortifino," Casey countered quickly to what he presumed was a protest from Bailey. "It's almost lunch time. What do you say?" He continued.

"Honestly," Bailey began, "I can't; I need to finalize Summerfest's vendors and guest list. I don't have time." Inside, Bailey was gushing like a schoolgirl. She had done her best not to give Casey the impression that she was interested in him. No, she could not do that. Besides, this was her job and her professional reputation on the line. The last thing Bailey wanted was for the wrong person to notice that she was mingling with the players, let alone her long-time crush, Casey Christopher.

Much to his dismay, Casey accepted Bailey's position. He didn't know if he could contain himself as he found her work ethic intriguing, almost to the point of turning him on.

"I dodged a bullet," Bailey texted Mina.

****

That night, Bailey found herself on the phone with one of her friends from high school, Nyhrie Dexter, to seek advice on how to deal with a professional athlete. "What do you think I should do, Nyh?"

"I don't know," Nyhrie answered, "It depends on what you want out of the situation." Bailey sat quietly to contemplate the question. "Who did you say the guy was again?" Nyhrie broke the silence over the phone.

"Casey. Casey Christopher, Bailey responded.

"Casey!" Nyhrie's response was not a question. "Do you mean Casey who was in last summer's Health and Fitness Body issue?"

"Uh," Bailey responded slowly, "Yeah, why? What's up?" Bailey quizzed.

"So now that I know who you are talking about, do you want my honest feedback, or do you want me to say something you want to hear?" Nyhrie was known amongst her friends as a straight shooter who does not hold anything back. Nyhrie's honesty was the reason people loved and hated talking to her.

Bracing herself for what her friend had to say, Bailey answered, "Give it to me straight."

"Girl," Nyhrie started, "I see why you have it bad for Casey, and I am not surprised that he would be pursuing someone like you but," Nyhrie paused, "From what I know, I hear he is practically married with a child. I think, a son."

Bailey's heart hit the floor when Nyhrie informed her of Casey's wife and kid. She was upset with herself for not knowing the status of his relationship. Bailey gathered her composure before speaking again, doing her best not to sound heartbroken. "I had no idea that he was in a relationship," Bailey started, "he has got to be out of his mind if he thinks I am going to be a side chick. I am beyond offended."

Bailey and Nyhrie were on the phone a few moments more before Nyhrie had to end the call. The Pacific/Eastern time difference made it difficult for the two to talk regularly. Bailey was happy that night her friend had a few minutes to spare and provide insight into the situation between herself and Mr. Christopher.

Monica

"What do you mean 'we' need to move, Casey?" Monica was taken entirely off guard when she woke up early Tuesday morning.

"Like I said, we need to move. This relationship is not working, and I can't do this with you anymore," Casey replied calmly.

"The hell you mean, you're not happy! Who is she?" Monica was furious; after all, she had given up so that Casey could excel, and suddenly, out of the blue, he wanted to end the relationship.

"There's no other woman," Casey lied.

"You must think I am a fool!" Monica paced across the bedroom as Casey sat on the edge of their king-sized bed. "You are a pathetic son of a…"

"Watch your mouth," Casey growled, halting Monica in her tracks. "I have never disrespected you or called you out of your name nor will you speak to me in that manner."

"You've got to be fucking kidding me?" Monica guffawed, "Don't patronize me, Casey! How the hell do you wake up and decide that our relationship is no longer convenient for you? What about our son?"

Monica was outraged; she had given up so much to be with Casey, including attending law school. She was the consummate football wife, though she had no ring. Monica made Casey's life as comfortable as possible. She was by his side during the high and low times, and now he wanted out.

Monica's mother had warned her about moving to California to "chase after some man." Monica had to admit that her mother may have been right. Now a single mother with no family or employment history, what was she to do? "This can't be my life," Monica mumbled as she made coffee. It was seven in the morning, which meant Josiah would wake in an hour. Marching up to the room she shared with Casey, coffee in hand, Monica slammed the door behind her.

"Casey!" Monica yelled as he emerged from the en suite bathroom.

"Yeah?" He answered, sounding unamused.

"What changed?" Monica asked tearfully.

"I wish I knew. I think we got too comfortable, and we lost ourselves in complacency." Monica rolled her eyes, "Look, I know this is a shock for you and I am sorry. I want to make this transition smooth for all of us, especially for Josiah."

"Don't try to sell me bullshit and call it rubies." Monica spat.

"I am looking for a condo downtown, and I am willing to temporarily foot the bill on a smaller house for you until we can come to a resolution. This house has been sold and we have thirty days to vacate."

"You piece of shit," Monica said as she walked across the room to Casey, "You had this planned all along and was going to leave me high and dry." Monica took a sip from the hot liquid to cool her temper. It didn't work; before she knew it, she heard Casey screaming out in agony as he used the bottom of his white crew neck shirt to wipe the coffee from his face.

Clenching his jaw, Casey returned to the bathroom, "You are tripping," he shouted.

****

Monica was in a rage; never in a million years had she thought Casey would leave her. She walked from room to room with Casey's Derek Jeter autographed Louisville Slugger, causing mayhem. She destroyed Casey's media room, his man cave was destroyed, his art room was damaged, all of his novelty pieces around the house had a personal meeting with the bat she clutched tightly. As Monica paced back to the room she and Casey shared, she devised another great idea. Walking past Casey's closet, she went to their bathroom to turn on the Jacuzzi tub. Leaving briefly, Monica returned with a handful of Casey's shoes, clothes, and jewelry. Leaving the room again, Monica headed down the hall to the laundry room. Opening the cabinet, she found exactly what she was looking for. She grabbed the two bottles of bleach and returned to the master bathroom. Monica emptied the contents of the first bottle of bleach, which was halfway empty. Walking back to Casey's closet, Monica grabbed Casey's most expensive suits. Unloading them in the tub with some of his other favorite items, she emptied the second 128 ounces of bleach.

Mildly satisfied, Monica went to her closet, where she grabbed her Modern Creation Munich travel bag and backpack. She stuffed clothes and shoes into the travel bag until it reached capacity. She placed her toiletries, computer, iPad, and related chargers in the backpack. Before closing the backpack, Monica went to the home office to secure the last items she would need for her departure. Unlocking the safe, Monica grabbed the three stacks of 100-dollar bills, each totaling ten thousand dollars. Next, she grabbed the birth certificates and social security cards for Josiah, herself, and Casey and placed them in a manila envelope for safe keeping.

Monica placed her bags by the top of the stairs before heading to Josiah's room to get him ready. Wiping the tears from her eyes, Monica attempted to put on her happy face. "JoJo, wake up, sweet pea," she whispered to her sleeping cherub. Josiah stirred as he rolled away from his mother. "JoJo," Monica started as she pulled the cover from her sleeping angel, "we have to go." The boy was unyielding. No longer willing to wait, Monica scooped the boy out of the bed, placed him on his feet, and guided him down the hall to his bathroom. Monica shared her agenda to get him excited enough to get ready quickly. As the five-year-old slowly took care of business in the bathroom, Monica hurriedly packed his Thomas the Train overnight bag with shoes and clothes, adding it to the bags at the top of the stairs.

"Come on, Jo, let Mommy put your clothes on." Being a mother left little time for Monica to nurture her broken heart. Josiah did not ask to be born; her troubles were not his to hold. As much as Monica wanted to sit in the corner and cry, she did not have time, nor did she want her son to see her in such a condition.

Grabbing the bags, she left at the top of the stairs, Monica waited for Josiah to get halfway down the steps before she started her descent. Opening the door to the garage, Monica observed the vehicle options, assessing which one would provide the maximum amount of comfort on their journey. Lifting the keys off the key hanger, she unlocked the doors to the silver Mercedes ML350. Monica ushered her son into his booster seat before loading their bags in the rear. "Are we going to see daddy before we leave?" An innocent Josiah asked.

"I'm afraid not, he's at work." Monica responded as she tucked a stray strand of hair behind her ear.

"Won't you miss daddy while we're gone? I am." Josiah admitted to his mother.

"It's okay, JoJo, we'll facetime him later on." As much as she hated Casey at that moment, Monica could never deny her child his father, even if he was a lying, selfish piece of shit.

"Yay!" Josiah yelled from the back seat of the SUV.

Maneuvering the vehicle from the garage, Monica asked Josiah if he was ready for their adventure. Luckily for her, he was and talked nonstop about his plans.

Casey

Casey was livid when he made it back home. Sure, he announced that the house he and Monica were living in was sold, and perhaps it was inconsiderate to share that he wanted to end the relationship simultaneously. Still, he never thought Monica would jump state, with his son no less.

Casey's anger skyrocketed when he made it into the house. "That girl is crazy!" he mumbled as he walked from room to room in the seven-room mansion. Casey nearly passed out when he went to use the restroom. His Tom Ford shoes, Armani, and Ferragamo suits all floated in a bleach bath. Dipping his hand in the tub to unplug the stopper, Casey felt a hard item at the bottom. Grabbing the hand towel off the rack, he wiped his hands as he ran to his closet. "No. No. No." He whined as he made his way back to the bathroom. Bending down next to the tub, he felt for the item again. Lifting the $85,000 watch from the tub that was now ruined by water and bleach, Casey angrily threw the worthless accessory down to the bathroom floor.

Having reached his breaking point, Casey grabbed his phone to call his mom. "Mom!" Casey said with haste as his mother, Janette, answered the phone.

"Casey is that you?" she asked.

"Yeah, it's me." he sulked.

Janette knew something was wrong with her youngest son by the tone of his voice. "What's wrong, baby?" she asked.

"Monica has gone crazy," he blamed, "I told her that I wanted to end the relationship and that we had thirty days to move because the house was sold."

"Okay," Janette said, providing verbal feedback.

"She trashed my house! I don't know how much money she caused me in damages, but this place is a mess and the crazy bi…"

"Watch your mouth," the older woman snapped.

"Chick," Casey sighed, "that crazy chick, bleached my most expensive clothes and shoes, including my Piguet watches."

"Those are only things, Casey." Janette reassured her seething son.

"My things, mom! She had no right to trash my house and clothes."

Janette loved her children just as much as any mother, but she did not sugarcoat the world for them. If they were wrong, she did not hesitate to tell them so. "Where is Josiah," Janette asked.

"I don't know, somewhere on the I-10 heading to Houston."

"Now you ought to be ashamed of yourself Casey James Christopher!" Janette exclaimed. "Now you're out here acting like the world is almost over because of things, things little boy. Meanwhile, your son is God knows where." Janette paused before continuing. "You are more concerned about your expensive toys than the safety of your child. I am truly disappointed in you." Casey hated disappointing his mother, and her words made him feel worse than he already did.

"Now I get that you are a famous football player," Janette continued, "but you are my son first, and I did not raise you to be selfish and inconsiderate. For one second, have you considered Monica's feelings?"

"No," Casey answered honestly.

"That girl traveled with you to California and took good care of you, and you mean to tell me that you woke up and decided you no longer wanted to be with the woman you had a child with?" There was a pause before Casey's mother continued, "If your father was alive today, what would he say?"

That was the million-dollar question that brought Casey to tears. His father, James Christopher, was a proud man who worked two jobs to provide for his family. He raised his five children, Janine, James Jr., Erica, Michelle, and Casey, to be upstanding people with high moral character and integrity. If Casey knew one thing, he knew his father would frown on this entire situation with Monica. James died of a massive heart attack when Casey was a senior in college. Before he passed, James told his son to keep an eye on Monica and to let her go if he was not serious about her. Casey ignored his father's advice, being the kid he was, and now, nearly ten years later, he found himself in a mess.

"Are you there?" Janette's voice broke through Casey's thoughts.

"Yeah, mom, I'm still here," he responded.

"Well, I'm going to call Monica to check in with her and see how my grandbaby is doing since you are too busy crying over shoes and things."

"Thanks, I appreciate that." Casey responded.

"Boy, I'm not doing that for you. I don't know what's wrong with you!" Janette sighed. "Listen, no matter what happens between you and Monica, you are still responsible for the care of Josiah. Do you hear me?"

"Yes, ma'am."

"You will not leave Monica out there to be a single mother to struggle and raise him on her own. So do whatever you need to do, to figure it out, and fast!"

"Okay, Mom," Casey answered, rolling his eyes.

"And, if you roll your eyes at me again, I will reach through the phone and give you a good whacking." The sassy woman responded.

Casey was amazed at how well his mother knew him, some 2,000 miles away. "Thanks, Mom; I love you and will talk to you later."

Bailey

Bailey found herself working on Independence Day; she and ninety-five percent of the Oilers staff had the day off. However, being new on the marketing team and wanting to make a good impression, Bailey decided to work that Friday morning. She planned on working until noon or so, at which point she would stop by a friend's party that she halfheartedly wanted to attend.

Oilers Central was virtually dead. Every now and again, Bailey would hear someone enter the sales and marketing pod. The solitude was a welcomed gift; Bailey could be much more creative without all the office buzz. Having completed her 'To Do' list sooner than expected, Bailey left the office early.

She took the south wing stairs and walked towards the exit for the employee parking lot. Crossing the parking lot, Bailey typed a message to send a friend when she heard a car sound its horn. Bailey waved her hand at the driver in the blacked-out luxury vehicle in an attempt to apologize for her pedestrian infraction. The driver sounded the horn again. "I'm going…sheesh!" She said aloud now annoyed by the driver's impatience.

"You better watch out there, little lady. Haven't you heard that it is illegal to text and walk?" The driver chastised.

"Very funny. Don't you know it is a holiday and you should not be here?" Bailey responded by looking up from her phone to match the driver's sarcasm.

"Yeah, well, I figured I'd get a workout in before heading to my bro's bar-b-que." Casey responded.

Remembering her conversation with Nyhrie a while ago, Bailey tried to cut the current discussion short. "Well, enjoy your day," Bailey waved as she dashed to her car. Hearing a car door shut behind her, Bailey knew that she had not escaped and needed to devise a plan quickly to escape the situation. Turning abruptly, Bailey was shocked to see how close Casey was to her. His presence felt so good, Bailey thought to herself. Snap out of it, she quickly admonished herself for having such thoughts about a married man. "Look, Casey," Bailey started, "this cat and mouse thing has to stop."

"What do you mean?" he asked sincerely.

"You," Bailey started, taking a step back. "I can tell that you are interested in me, and like I said before, I have a professional reputation to worry about," crossing her arms in front of her chest, Bailey continued, "and you, you have a wife and child, and should be ashamed of yourself for even looking at other women." Before allowing Casey to respond, Bailey turned and sashayed to her car, feeling satisfied. Bailey – 1, Casey – 0.

****

"What's wrong with you?" Sierra asked, passing Bailey a chilled beer.

"Oh, nothing much," Bailey lied. Bailey met Sierra when she joined her sorority's San Diego area chapter. Sierra was one of a few younger members in the chapter, and she and Bailey hit it off immediately.

"Girl," Sierra started, "I know your butt isn't okay." Bailey enjoyed Sierra; however, with their new friendship, she was still determining how much of her business she should divulge.

"It's not a big deal, plus more guests are sure to be arriving soon," Bailey responded, "Let's do lunch Sunday, and I'll fill you in." Bailey had hoped this would ease her friend's curiosity for the day.

Satisfied with Bailey's response, "Gusto's at 11:30", Sierra responded. Changing the subject, Sierra shared what she believed to be good news with Bailey. "Corey's friend, Mike is supposed to be coming today".

"Okay," Bailey replied, trying to play it cool.

"You are such a fraud!" Sierra teased, "You're over there trying to act like you are not phased. Last time you came with me to support Corey and his bowling team you had plenty of questions about Mike, and now you are trying to sit there and act like you don't know about him".

"It's not like that", Bailey started.

"Then, what is it like?" Sierra quizzed.

Sighing, Bailey did not anticipate an interrogation; desperately trying to change the subject, she asked, "Have you heard any more details about the Pearls Project?"

"Don't try to change the subject on me," Sierra quipped, "but to answer your question, no, I haven't heard any updates outside of the date and location of the event."

Monica

"What am I supposed to do?" A weeping Monica asked her younger sister, Sharmaine, "I gave up everything to be with him," she continued.

Sharmaine was Monica's bold little sister who held a lot of love for her older sister. Though the pair were five years apart, their bond was that of Irish twins. Sharmaine paused to consider her words wisely, "You know, mom and I didn't think it was a good idea for you to move to California with Casey. I'm not sure what you want me to say but let me know how to help."

Monica sat in the corner of her sister's large sectional sofa. As she surveyed the living room, Monica felt a twinge of resentment from everything her younger sister had accomplished, alone. Sharmaine managed to graduate from the University of Houston with a bachelor's and master's degree in business in just five years before landing a project manager job for a well-respected organization. Sharmaine was a homeowner and currently working her way up the corporate ladder.

Monica was proud of her baby sister but could not help but feel bad for squandering her own opportunities. Before graduating, Monica was accepted into three law schools and was waiting for a few more offers. Instead of pursuing her passion for interpreting the law, Monica became the quintessential football girlfriend. Now, here she was in her sister's house without a thing. Monica did have Josiah; however, she did not have a way to care for him properly. "How could I let this happen?" Monica mumbled.

"What was that?" Sharmaine inquired.

"Oh, I was thinking out loud," Monica answered.

"I spoke to Mom the other day," Sharmaine paused, "and she is concerned about you."

"I know. I tried to reassure her that I was fine." Monica followed.

"She and Pops are supposed to move down here after he retires next year," Sharmaine shared.

"That'll be great! Maybe JoJo and I could start over down here. I can look for work as… as something," a melancholic Monica concluded.

****

Monica was sick; after settling into her sister's massive home, she cried herself to sleep every night, only to wake up with more tears and puffy eyes. Monica's saving grace was her son, and luckily for her, Sharmaine's home was large enough that her son could continue to have his own room across the hall from her. Every morning, Monica allowed her son to call his father because, after all, this was the longest and furthest they had been apart from each other. As much as Monica wanted to hate Casey and forget he existed, her son reminded her of the love they once shared.

After two weeks in Houston, Monica decided that she had wallowed in self-pity long enough. On a record-high July afternoon, Monica decided to retake control of her life and begin planning for life as a single mother. That was the most complex realization she had to face. Monica never imagined that she would be a single mother or imagined life without Casey, yet they were now a reality. She decided the best decision would be to make Houston her new home since her sister already lived there, and her parents would be moving to the area shortly. Raising a child, especially a male child, would require a village, and Monica could not think of a better support system than that of her family.

On this summer day, Monica decided to stop thinking and start doing. First, she researched preschools for Josiah, followed by searching for Public Policy and Public Administration master programs for herself. The next item on Monica's agenda was finding a family attorney in San Diego to legalize custody and parental responsibilities. Monica knew she had no employable skills and had only so much money saved, but she knew if she wanted to live independently and return to school, she would need financial support from Casey.

Bailey

Bailey was excited to meet her friend Sierra for lunch after what turned out to be an epic Independence Day party. On Friday, Bailey reluctantly attended Sierra's party, and much to her surprise, the gathering was far more eventful than she imagined. Mike, Corey's friend, was the center of attention, captivating an audience of ogling female admirers. Bailey watched as Mike entertained the room with his adventurous stories and noted the awkwardness of his infectious laugh. Before the night was over, Mike made it his mission to steal a few moments of Bailey's time. Though she did not join his fan club, he occasionally noticed her staring at him from across the room.

"Are you enjoying yourself, Miss Bailey?" Mike asked as he crossed the threshold of the sliding door separating the patio and the living room. Bailey watched as Mike crossed the deck and sat across from her before responding.

"I must admit, I had more fun than I thought I would," Bailey responded honestly.

"Had?" Mike asked, perplexed and with a half-smile. Bailey sensed a deeper meaning to his question but opted to respond to the question and not Mike's implication.

"Yes, had," Bailey started, "Sierra and Corey certainly know how to throw a party. The weather was nice, the music was vibing, and the fireworks were a perfect exclamation to a very chill day. I'm not sure if you noticed or not, but people are beginning to leave. The only reason that I have not made a B-line for the door is because I promised to help clean up."

"Is that right?" Mike inquired as he adjusted his seat. "You must not know Corey and Sierra very well. Do not let the thinning crowd fool you. The party is just getting started".

"Is that right?" Bailey asked, taking a sip of the white wine from the wine glass she was holding.

"Oh, most definitely!" Mike responded, "I didn't come out here to talk about the hosts though." Placing her wine glass on the patio table, which separated Mike and her, Bailey proceeded to lock eyes with the man she found herself grossly attracted to.

"So, what did you come out here to talk about then?" she asked.

****

"Hey girl, hey!" Sierra squealed as her friend approached the ocean-view table where she had been waiting.

As the ladies separated from their embrace, Bailey responded, "Hey," as she removed her purse from her shoulder and placed it on the chair to the left of where her friend was initially seated.

Sierra was excited to be able to speak with her friend finally. Often, work-life kept them both occupied, but Sierra was aching to know what happened between her friend and Mike. "How is Mike doing?" Sierra asked immediately.

Taken aback by Sierra's forwardness, Bailey tried to compose herself, "Well, I see you are not wasting any time."

"Not at all," Sierra retorted. "All I know is you, and Mike ditched my party to cozy up outside on the patio."

Bailey started to open her mouth to speak but was quickly interrupted by her friend, "…, and before you get to denying anything, I practically watched you all night. I mean we were playing Spades and Dominoes, and Mike loves Dominoes, but did he come in to play after Corey went out to get him? Nope!" Taking a small sip of water, Sierra continued, "So, let me ask you again, how is Mike doing?"

"Well," Bailey began as she chuckled at her friend, "I see you're concerned about Mike, but I'm doing quite fine, thanks for asking." Bailey dodged the balled-up straw wrapping paper Sierra threw at her for teasing. "No, but seriously, we haven't really spoken all like that, but I assume he is all right."

"Hmph," Sierra retorted, "According to Corey, Mike is really smitten with you."

"Is that right?" Bailey queried, "What did Mike tell Corey?"

"Yes, girl!"

"Well, I find that interesting since he hasn't asked me out on a proper date yet." Bailey shared.

Sierra shared encouraging words with her friend, "Be patient with him, he can be an oddball sometimes. How about I tell Core..."

"No!" Bailey exclaimed. "I do not want you or Corey coaching Mike. If he wants to take me on a date, he'll ask."

The two ladies continued their lively discussion over their entrees and cocktails before departing the restaurant and making plans to connect again, soon.

Casey

"John, I just want to ensure that my son is properly cared for, and I'm not trying to have the courts all in my business." Casey was silent as his attorney, John Marquette, responded to his request. "Paying for my son's education, health and daycare is not a problem. I don't want his mother struggling to care for him. They're in Texas now, so the cost of living shouldn't be so high." Casey paused again to listen to his attorney. "Listen, this is what I want to do, if we take out the cost of care and education, seven racks should be more than enough for shelter, food, and clothing. She has my truck, so she doesn't need transportation."

Casey understood that he did not end things the best way with Monica, and while he no longer held romantic feelings for her, he had love for her as the mother of his child. He hoped that the two could be friends and co-parent amicably someday. In the meantime, he wanted to ensure that his child was okay, and setting up a financial agreement with Monica was the best way to do so.

✱✱✱✱✱✱✱✱✱✱✱✱✱✱✱✱✱✱✱✱

The plane ride from New York was lively for the Oilers because they'd just beat the Gotham in their pre-season opener. As their teammates played pranks on one another and joked around, Casey and Jamal sat in the middle of the aircraft playing Gin Rummy. "What's going on with that redbone from upstairs?" Jamal asked as he shuffled the deck of cards.

"Man, nothing," Casey began, "She keeps trying to give me the cold shoulder. I know she's feeling me, though. I can see it in her eyes."

"Is that right?" Jamal asked, laughing.

"Have you seen me? What woman in her right mind wouldn't want ya boy?" Casey responded.

Staring at the cards in his hands, "The way you dropped Monica I can imagine plenty of women who wouldn't want you… starting with Monica," Jamal replied.

"Did you really have to go there?" Casey asked, sulking back in his seat.

"Of course, I did." Jamal started. "You walk around like some sort of Casanova. Fool you ain't Gerald Levert!"

"Ouch!" Casey responded.

"Am I lying?" Jamal asked.

"Man, whatever," Casey said as he played his turn, "it's your turn to play." Jamal had struck a nerve with Casey. Casey knew he had not managed things well with Monica; his mom had already scolded him. Now he was hearing about his character flaws from one of his best friends. The truth was not pretty, and it hurt. Searching for his phone in his duffle bag in the seat next to him, Casey unlocked the screen saver and tapped the icon for his text messages. Opening a new message, Casey proceeded to type a lengthy message. "Who is this?" the 4-1-5 number responded. He replied "Casey Christopher" to the message. To avoid further embarrassment, Casey turned his phone off for the remainder of the flight.

Casey knew that with the regular season quickly approaching, he had to get his life under control because nothing was going right for him. He had not seen his son in over a month, and Monica needed to cooperate more. To make matters worse, the young lady he had his eye on wholly ignored him and any attempt he made to get better acquainted. After he poured out his heart via text message, he had not heard from Bailey, and it appeared that she was making every effort possible to ignore him. Casey was at a loss, football was the only thing he recognized and he needed to keep that one thing in his life in order since everything else was not.

Bailey

Bailey and Mike had gone out on several dates since Bailey last spoke to Sierra. She had not confronted Mike for ghosting her the week after they met because she had resolved that any guy genuinely interested in her would say so. Bailey held no complaints about Mike; he was a great guy, they had a lot of fun together, and she genuinely enjoyed his company. One thing Bailey never tolerated was being treated less than the lady she was. Being the only girl with an overprotective father and brothers spoiled would be an understatement to describe Bailey, though she did not act like an entitled brat.

Rereading the text message she received from an unknown number, Bailey was in an emotional spiral when she inquired about who the messenger was. Of all the people, Bailey did not tag Casey to be a forthcoming guy in a situation that did not require him to do so. Scrolling back to the top of the message, Bailey began to reread it:

Bailey,

I can't go another day without telling you how I feel. I know that we have not spent a significant amount of time *together, but your energy is magnetic, and I can't help but want to be near you. I've watched how you carried yourself in several situations, and you are one bad mamma jamma! *Great, now I sound like my pops when he would talk to my mama.* I know you might find it hard to believe that I dig you, but I assure you I would not have gone through hell and high water to get your number. I want to keep it 100 with you so there will be no misunderstandings. 1) I am single. I recently ended a relationship with a woman I've been with since college. It did not end well, but I am committed to caring for my son. She no longer lives in Cali, and we're trying to figure out how to move on and what is best for my son. 2) My son is the only child I have. There are no random baby mamas out there. 3) I don't do drugs or have a drinking problem. – Or gambling. 4) I go to church as much as possible in the off-season. I think it's pretty apparent why I miss church at the end of the year ;-) 5) My life is an open book, and I want you to feel comfortable to ask me anything you'd like. I'm returning from New York and want to take you out on Tuesday. Let me know. Please say yes!*

Bailey needed to figure out what to do after discovering the 4-page letter was from thee Casey Christopher of the San Diego Oilers. He could have any woman he wants; for crying out loud, he could probably snap his fingers and be back with his college sweetheart. "What does he want from me?" Bailey asked herself as she got up from the couch to pace the living room floor. A part of Bailey wanted to meet up with Casey to get the answers for herself, not to mention that he was her crush, so any time she was around him felt like magic.

Monday was ending, and Bailey knew the window was nearing for appropriate texting hours; she either had to respond soon or ignore his message altogether. In a last impulsive moment, Bailey raced to her couch to pick up her phone to respond to the text. "Time? Location? I'll meet you there", was all she could manage.

****

After work on Tuesday Bailey commenced the 30-minute drive to Scripps Beach. She did not understand why Casey would choose a beach for a "date" when they could have gone to plenty of places in the Gaslamp or downtown. Alas, she was driving north to La Jolla to meet this man.

To calm her nerves, Bailey listened to Trina's third album, "Glamorest Life." The slick rap lyrics had a calming effect on Bailey, and she could groove to the rappers' wild songs and mesmerizing beats. Plus, she would need reassurance that she could not be affected by any man, even if he was her longtime crush, Casey Christopher, star of the San Diego Oilers. Bobbing her head to "I Gotta," Bailey pulled into the Scripps Beach parking lot; it had been a record hot day, so parking was at a premium with beach goers seeking reprieve from the heat. She imagined the beach would be filled with surfers itching for a swim before dusk set in, she did not account for there to be so many families with small children still out.

Bailey managed to find a parking spot close to the beach entrance; she backed her red Charger between two midsize sedans. Before exiting her car, Bailey reapplied her tinted lip gloss with glitter, finger combed and fluffed her bob hairstyle and popped two icebreaker mints in her mouth. She did not know what to expect, and while she didn't want to put in too much effort, she did not want to go out on the beach looking crazy. Walking to the back of her car, Bailey opened the trunk to replace her four-inch nude-colored stilettos with a pair of black thong sandals adorned with rhinestones. The sandals paired well enough with her tan cap-sleeve shift dress with flowers in various shades of blue. Bailey closed the trunk and went to open the passenger's side backdoor to grab her Black Vince Camuto crossbody purse. As she walked across the parking lot towards the beach entrance, Bailey texted the unsaved number, "Where are you?"

Casey

Casey could not remember the last time he had been this nervous; his palms were sweaty, and his mind was racing. "What have I gotten myself into?" Casey scolded himself. "Maybe she will not come." He continued chastising himself with claims that it took Bailey more than a day to respond to his invitation. As Casey was on the verge of another negative thought, his cell phone buzzed in his pants pocket. "Showtime," Casey said to himself as he began to walk toward the steps for the beach entrance from the beach to the parking lot to greet his date for the evening.

Bailey looked gorgeous, Casey thought to himself. "Hi, beautiful," Casey said as he closed the gap between himself and Bailey. Feeling a sense of calmness, Casey opened his arms and asked for a hug. He noticed Bailey's slight hesitation before she silently moved toward him to oblige his request. She felt so good in his arms that Casey did not want to let her go, but ultimately, he released his arms as he felt her take a step back. "You smell nice," Bailey commented.

"Well, I would hope so," Casey chided. "Thank you…. It's Polo Double Black."

Rolling her eyes, Bailey stifled her amusement as she brushed by Casey, "So, why did you have me drive all the way out to La Jolla?"

"Be- because it's peaceful out here. I like to come out here when I want to think or clear my head," Casey responded honestly. "I'm happy you accepted my invitation. I was afraid that you wouldn't show up," he continued.

"To be honest, I was on the fence as to whether or not I should respond to your text, but then I figured a free meal wouldn't hurt," Bailey laughed, "Clearly, I was mistaken since we're not at some fancy 5-star restaurant".

Bailey's words had struck a nerve; did he come across as one-dimensional? Why couldn't he enjoy the calmness and serenity of the beach? Casey took a deep-sea salt breath, destined not to be unraveled by his date. "Let's make our way down these stairs," Casey said as he held out his hand for Bailey to place her hand in his. When they reached the bottom step where the sand kissed their feet,

Casey could feel Bailey squeeze his hand as he led her to a tent two hundred feet from the beach entrance.

The tent was an enclosed structure with a zippered entrance that Casey had set up earlier that afternoon. Inside the tent sat a table set for two with two dozen red roses in the center. "Hmmm, this is interesting," Bailey said as she walked to the table to inspect the roses. Casey 1stood at the tent's entrance as he watched her pluck the card from the roses and read it silently to herself. When Bailey turned to face Casey, he swore he saw a glimmer of hope in her eyes, or it could have been the hope in his heart. "You're welcome," Bailey said sweetly, responding to the message in the card she just read.

Re-orienting himself to this moment, Casey moved towards Bailey to pull out her chair for her to sit. Before taking his seat, Casey went to a cooler in the corner of the tent to pull out five gourmet deli sandwiches for Bailey to choose from. "There's turkey, ham, roast beef, veggie, and tuna here for you to choose from. I know this isn't Morton's or anything, but the place I got these from is legit," Casey said nervously.

"Which one are you having?" Bailey quizzed.

"One of the four you don't pick," Casey said, matching Bailey's stare-down. After what felt like eons, Bailey finally reached for the turkey sandwich, and Casey returned to breathing. He sat the roast beef sandwich on his plate and then grabbed the remaining three sandwiches to place back in the cooler. From the cooler, he pulled out a bottle of sparkling apple cider and a bag of Cooler Ranch Doritos. "Shall we?" Casey asked as he opened the bag of chips and cider.

"We shall," Bailey responded, blushing.

Monica

Monica's flight into San Diego International Airport from Houston was delayed for half an hour when it landed at a quarter past eleven on Thursday morning. Monica had been seething when her friend Kim told her that Casey had started dating. It had barely been two months since Casey announced that he was leaving her, and though she knew deep in her heart that the relationship was over, there was an ounce of hope she held that he would try to reconcile their relationship. Monica was outraged that Casey could move on with his life without any thought or regard for her or their son. On top of that, Monica was suspicious that Casey had left her for another woman.

Luckily, Monica found a cheap ticket to San Diego, and her sister was willing to watch Josiah for the weekend. She was determined to get answers from Casey now that she had time to confront him. When Casey initially broke the news to Monica, she did not want to cause a scene that could possibly traumatize her son, nor did she think a phone call would be a sufficient method for saying her peace. As she walked to the baggage claim, Monica texted an all too familiar number, "We need to talk, NOW!"

Seconds after Monica pressed the send button, her phone started singing the chorus to Kelis' "Caught Out There," signaling a call from her son's father. "What?" Monica answered, failing to employ proper telephone etiquette.

"You said you wanted to talk, so I called you. Is everything ok with JoJo?" Casey asked. Monica could not help but feel a twinge of sadness when Casey did not ask how she was doing. Gathering her thoughts, Monica replied, "Josiah is fine, he's with my sister. I wanted to square a few things away with you while I'm here in San Diego for the weekend. I'll be staying at the Gaslamp Hilton and can meet you at 7pm at the seafood place I like on 5th Ave."

"Ahhh, tonight is not good for me," Casey admitted, "Is there any way we could meet for breakfast or lunch tomorrow?" he asked.

Monica found her blood pressure rising as the father of her child tried to negotiate a meeting around what she believed to be pre-planned dates. "Nope", Monica responded indignantly, "It's about *our* son and you need to talk to me if you want to stay off of child support."

Casey sighed deeply before responding, "Don't threaten me. You was the one who decided to leave for another state and take *my* son with you! It is never a problem for me to speak with you, especially when it comes to Josiah." Casey paused momentarily before continuing, "I don't appreciate you coming back to San Diego making demands like I owe you something. I have other things I need to do, and the way you are coming at me ain't cool." Casey was upset that Monica would return to town, trying to call the shots and dictate his life. However, he knew he would never snuff Monica, especially if Josiah were the topic of discussion.

"So, are you meeting me tonight, or what?" Monica asked.

****

Despite her hotel being within walking distance, Monica purposefully arrived late to Rockin' Lobster. Monica knew Casey would be agitated by her delay, but she did everything possible to maintain the advantage. It had been weeks since Casey had announced that he was ending the relationship, and that was the last time she had seen him in person. When she walked in, Monica scanned the restaurant from the entrance; moments later, she located him at the bar watching one of the televisions broadcasting sports news. "Hey, big head!" Monica greeted Casey as she gently smacked him on his head.

"You're late," Casey responded without facing his guest.

"Yeah, well, I'm here now. Don't be such a grump," Monica cajoled, "Let's grab a seat."
Casey slowly rose from his seat, turned towards Monica, and opened his arms to hug her.

"You look nice," Casey complemented. Monica dressed in funeral black. She wore five-inch peep toe booties, black skinny jeans, and a long-sleeved black collar shirt.

"You don't look so bad yourself," Monica chided as Casey dressed in grey San Diego Oilers cotton sweatpants and a hoodie.

Monica found a booth near the restaurant's entrance where they could have their privacy and be amongst the chaos. If things went awry, she wanted to have a distraction. "Casey," Monica began, "thank you for meeting with me on short notice; I really do appreciate it."

"You didn't leave me much choice, did you," Casey sneered.

Monica felt her heart sink at Casey's response. She could not believe that he was over her. After nearly ten years and a child later, it was hard for Monica to imagine that Casey could move on so effortlessly. She thought that Casey perhaps had been cheating on her and that she somehow missed the signs like an idiot. "Well," Monica started to regain her composure, "I do appreciate your time and wanted to meet with you in person to discuss next steps."

No matter how angry Casey made Monica, she knew that she would never deprive her son of his father, even if he were a lying, cheating son of a bitch. If for nothing else, Casey was a great father. "For the foreseeable future Josiah and I will be living in Texas. That is where I have the most support and the cost of living is cheaper. I know football season is just around the corner and Josiah has been asking about you. I'm more than willing on occasion to bring him out to San Diego, but I would like to schedule your time to see Josiah."

"Schedule time to see my own son, Monica? Really?" Casey responded, "Had you not run away, I could see my son whenever and not through video chat."

"Yes, well," Monica started, "had you not announced like an award show that you were selling the home our family shared and cowardly ended our relationship, I would not have had to leave." She paused momentarily before continuing, "But, we are not here to discuss our failed relationship and the events surrounding it. We are here to discuss how you can maintain an active position in his life despite being thousands of miles away."

"That is one thing we can agree on, I will be present in my son's life," Casey said definitively.

"And," Monica interrupted, "I know you are an amazing man and father; and if possible, I would like to keep the courts and attorneys out of this".

"What exactly are you saying?" Casey asked.

"Your attorneys have been in contact with me, and I find it ridiculous that the two of us can't come together to figure this out ourselves," Monica answered.

Casey took a few moments to process what Monica suggested before responding, "It sounds like you have been thinking about this for a while, what does this arrangement look like to you?" Casey quizzed.

"Raising a child requires more than money, they need nurturing and guidance as well." Monica started. "For obvious reasons, I will be Josiah's primary care provider, and living in Texas allows me to draw on the support of my family. I was accepted into an accelerated master's program and will be done next December."

"Congratulations," Casey interrupted.

"Thank you," Monica responded, "For the next two years, and we can renegotiate after that time passes, you are one hundred percent responsible for Josiah's health insurance, tuition, and daycare, fifty percent responsible for average daily expenses, and pay for any travel necessary for in-person visits." Monica took a drink from the water the waiter had provided them with, "After I finish my program and find a job, I expect to split all living costs with you fifty-fifty, except for travel, which can get really expensive quickly."

"That's doable," Casey responded, "I'd also like to add that we celebrate his birthday together; I don't see why he needs to celebrate his birthday at two different times when his birthday is during my offseason. Holidays are going to be tricky since that is in the middle of my season. I cannot guarantee that I can be present if you don't travel to wherever I am, but I can be sure to video chat with him".

Monica smiled and nodded her head in agreement.

"And, lastly," Casey started again, "I would like Josiah with me during the summer."

Monica was shocked to find that Casey wanted to take her son for two months out of the year, and if she were honest with herself, she was unsure if she could manage to be away from JoJo for so long. Their agreement was acceptable until Casey wanted to play temporary full-time daddy during the summer.

"This agreement is for two years?" Monica asked.

"Two years from today," Casey responded, holding his pinky finger.

Wrapping her finger around his, Monica confirmed, "Two years it is."

Bailey

"I need some more wine," Bailey announced as she got up from the corner nook of her sectional couch where she was sitting to make her way to the kitchen.

"Good, you can refill my glass, too" Sierra responded as she stretched her arm to hand Bailey her wine glass.

The two women spent the afternoon engaging in girl talk and gossip accompanied by snacks and wine. Lots of wine. Bailey poured the remaining contents of the Stella Rosa Platinum into her wine glass before opening a new bottle to fill Sierra's glass. Bailey grabbed a bag of cheddar popcorn, placed the newly opened bottle of wine under her left arm, and picked up the two glasses as she walked back into the living room.

"I've been thinking about it," Bailey started as she handed Sierra her glass of wine, "Casey is a nice guy, but he has too much going on. He had to cancel on Friday because of some stuff with his son's mother."

"How long ago did you say they broke up?' Sierra asked.

"He told me about two months ago," Bailey responded.

"Hmm," Sierra started, "I would be careful if I were you. They've been together for hella long and have a child together; there's no telling what kind of bond they have." Sierra took a sip from her wine glass before continuing, "Trust me, you do not want to be left out looking like Boo Boo the Fool. Been there done that."

"I hear you. Believe me I do not want to be out here looking crazy. Plus, when you talk about that kind of history there's no competing."

"How is Mike?" Sierra asked, shifting the discussion from the football jock to her best friend by proxy.

"Mike is good. You know we've been kicking it here and there but nothing too serious," Bailey admitted.

"Well, you know he's feeling you and comes with none of the drama," Sierra said as she advocated for her friend.

"I know," Bailey started, "to be honest I'm not looking to settle down with any of these guys. They both have great personalities, and I am enjoying this season of dating."

"I don't know how you do it," Sierra admitted, "there is nothing more comforting to me than being in a relationship. I think I'm too awkward to be casually dating but, at least you have two decent guys in rotation."

"Yeah, I guess," Bailey smirked.

****

Bailey was excited about her new project; she was coordinating the player's and coaches' annual catalog that would be gifted to season ticket holders. Bailey knew the team catalog was essential for the Oilers organization and their fans. She would need to arrange a picture day with the media department for players and coaches to take their current profile pictures and meet with players so they could complete the questionnaires for their player biographies. During the department meeting, when they discussed the upcoming catalog and other open projects, Bailey suggested updating how they collected player and coach information. She had heard it was a nightmare to type in each person's information, especially since many wrote like a seven-year-old. Since the Oilers partnered with a major media company and had dozens of their tablets collecting dust in the closet, Bailey's simple suggestion of asking players and coaches to fill out their information on a tablet had won her the job.

The unique challenge of this project was its time-sensitive nature. The team wanted to have the catalog prepared for distribution by the first home game no later than the second. However, since the project started during training camp, the catalog could only be sent to the printer after the final 53-man roster was announced on the last day of camp. Luckily for her, the first round of player cuts had been completed, and the team was now operating on a 76-man roster instead of the beginning camp's 90-man roster. After assessing a few methods for collecting player data, she found creating a survey the most efficient method. All players and coaches needed to do was click the survey icon on the tablet's home screen, fill in their names, and complete the questionnaire. Once all the players and coaches completed the questionnaire, she could copy and paste their information into the catalog template. She would then insert the profile photo after she received it from the media department.

Bailey could only access fifty tablets in the marketing office, she would need more to have the entire training camp roster and coaching staff complete their questionnaires in one sitting. In preparation for multiple sessions, Bailey coordinated through the senior ranks to meet with the defensive, offensive, and special teams with their coaches during their specific meetings. No matter how often she interacted with the players and coaches, Bailey always felt nervous entering the classrooms where they met. She felt like she was invading their space, and today was no different.

The San Diego August heat was a scorcher. Though Bailey did not like walking around professional settings with her arms exposed, she knew there was no way she could wheel the cart containing the tablets in the cardigan sweater she had worn around the office to fight some of the chill from the air conditioning. The classrooms were behind the stadium where the Oilers played next to the practice field. Bailey had arrived at the classroom before the players arrived and was thankful for a moment to gather her thoughts and wipe the sweat from her forehead and top lip. The special teams unit was the first round of players and coaches she met with. Bailey gave her well-thought-out speech and instructions to the men, leaving them to complete the questionnaires without incident.

Bailey repeated the same spiel twice for the offensive and defensive teams, respectively. She was checking her email on one of the tablets when the silence was interrupted by a cough and "Excuse me" from one of the players. "Shit!" Bailey exclaimed under her breath. "Yes, sir, how can I help you?" she asked of one of the defensive players.

"Don't call me sir, Casey, will do." Bailey felt the piercing of his words and wondered why he sounded so agitated. She placed the tablet on the table in preparation for the gentlemen's comments.

"Yes, Casey, my apologies. If you are done with the questionnaire, you can leave it where you are seated, and I will come by to collect it later," Bailey smiled warmly, attempting to hide her discomfort.

"Actually, I am having a problem with this tablet and can't seem to figure it out." Casey's teammates and coaches now watched the exchange between Casey and the girl from the office, volleying between the two.

"Hmm, that is peculiar Bailey stated, "No one else seemed to have a problem with these tablets." Bailey grabbed an extra tablet from the cart and started it up as she went to the back of the classroom to swap tablets with Casey.

The Defensive Coordinator, Jack, was not a fan of the football business, especially when it interfered with the game and, more importantly, his practice. Jack sensed something was happening between the girl from the office and his star D-lineman and did not appreciate it. "It's been ten minutes already; how many of you are done?" Jack grumbled. Startled by Jack's outburst, Bailey was frozen at the end of the aisle where Casey was sitting and uncertain what to do.

"Yes, for those," Bailey stuttered, "For those of you who have completed the questionnaire be sure to press send and just leave the tablet right where you are sitting, and I'll collect them after you leave."

"You heard the little lady," Jack yelled out, "If you're done with this nonsense, leave your tablets and get back out there on the field." The silence was interrupted by players getting out of their chairs, moving around, and chattering. "For the rest of ya," Jack started, "you have five minutes to get back to the field!"

Only seven players remained in the classroom once everyone filed out. When Bailey finally reached Casey, she clicked on the questionnaire icon on the tablet she was holding before exchanging it for the tablet he held. Much to Bailey's surprise, Casey handed her his tablet and rejected the new one she had for him. A note was written on the tablet Casey gave Bailey, she read the note silently as Casey watched her. "Yo, dawg, you ready to bounce," a deep, husky voice broke through the silence. Bailey lifted her head from the note she was reading to see Eric Morgan facing her and Casey from where he was seated a few rows up; the remaining players had cleared the room.

"Not yet, E, give me a few minutes," Casey bargained. Bailey stepped back as Casey rose from his chair and stretched like a starfish.

Bailey quickly finished reading the note on the tablet before deleting it, "It seems that you were able to troubleshoot on your own, thank you for completing the questionnaire." Bailey said as she began collecting the tablets from the tabletops.

"You don't have anything else to say," Casey pressed.

"At the moment, no. I am at work and under a strict deadline," Bailey answered more harshly than she wanted. "Besides," Bailey continued, trying to soften her tone, "Your coach gave you five minutes, and you are way beyond that now."

"She's right, bro; we need to get going," Eric said.

"Yeah, bet," Casey responded, obviously annoyed by Bailey's lack of enthusiasm or response to his note.

Casey

Casey found himself back in the gym at ten at night for what would be his third workout of the day. He needed to let some steam off his chest because the week had not been very kind to him. Between Monica's demands and Bailey pretending he didn't exist; Casey did not know what to do with himself. For the first time since his father's death, Casey truly felt alone. The more Casey thought of his current situation, the harder he pumped the 400-pound barbell.

Exhausted, Casey replaced the equipment where he created his weightlifting circuit; he could not continue like this, overextending his body with intense physical workouts. Casey knew that he was trying to replace the chaos of his life with the gym. He knew it was time to address those things in his life that grieved him. Picking up his workout bag and his gallon jug of water from the floor, Casey exited the gym for his car. Since Monica took his Mercedes SUV when she left the state, Casey had been driving his all-black Mercedes AMG E series. While it's not his preferred daily vehicle, he did not want to purchase something else, he remotely opened the luxury vehicle's trunk and placed his gym bag and water in there; he closed the trunk and limped to the driver's side as he pulled his mobile phone out of his sweatpants pocket. Casey sank into the driver's seat, adjusting himself until he found a comfortable position. He scrolled through his phone, sending text messages to two contacts before turning the phone off and leaving the parking lot.

****

It had been months since Casey had last seen JoJo, and his heart smiled when he played with his son and heard him laugh with excitement. He and Monica had been separated for months, and Casey had been kind to her during the transition. Though Monica was not causing much grief, she had the one thing Casey could not readily access: their son, Josiah. Casey had vowed never to be a deadbeat father, and although he knew that he was failing to provide his son with the stable family like he had, Casey promised to be an integral part of his son's development.

After feeling miffed by Bailey and having to meet Monica's demands, Casey decided to make demands of his own for those things that mattered most to him. After a late-night gym session, Casey contacted his mother and Monica to prepare arrangements for Josiah to live in San Diego with his father for the remainder of summer. Monica had begun taking classes for an advanced degree in Houston, and with the regular season on the horizon, Casey wanted to spend as much time with Josiah as possible. While his busy schedule was not particularly conducive to that of a single father, Casey thanked God that he had a mother who loved him and was willing to put her life on pause to help care for JoJo.

"Let's go again!" an excited Josiah proclaimed as he hurried out of the ball pit of the giant slide, he and his father just came down. Casey was out of breath because of the fright he just experienced going down a slide that he did not believe was safe for kids. Since this was their first weekend together and Casey wanted to enjoy his son as much as possible, they made the trek to the stairs of the structure to climb to the highest platform for the slide.

Casey had allowed Josiah to take him on that slide three more times before redirecting his son's attention to other attractions at Adventure's Landing. If he were honest with himself, Casey did not have the energy to walk up the stairs- in football years, he was old. "I want to ride the cars," Josiah exclaimed as they walked by the ride's exit. "No problem, Champ, let's find where the line begins."

Casey allowed Josiah to play until the park shut down, and he was most pleased that Adventure's Landing closed at 8 pm on weekdays. Otherwise, they would have been there until 11pm had it been the weekend. On their way home, Casey let Josiah decide what they would eat for dinner. Luckily, the little guy had wanted In-N-Out, which was not too far from Casey's house and had a drive-thru, which was even more appealing to the exhausted father of one.

Monica

"Hey Casey, how is everything going?" Monica asked when the father of her child answered his phone.

"Everything is going well; Josiah is having a blast. Let me get him for you." Casey answered reassuringly. Monica's heart was tearing apart. How could she be with this man for nearly ten years, have a child with him, and almost marry? How could he be so calm and treat her like an ordinary friend? Her mind could not understand how he could break their family up. She knew it was ridiculous to continue to mourn her relationship with Casey, but he was her comforter, and now she felt like a stranger.

"Okay," was all Monica could muster as the lump in her throat grew and the muscles in her trachea stiffened. "I will not cry," she whispered while waiting for her son to get on the phone. Monica heard some ruffling just before the melodic sound of Josiah getting on the phone. "Hi, mama!" Josiah said excitedly.

"Hi baby, how are you?" Monica asked.

"Momma, I'm having so much fun with Daddy! We went to a park where they have this big slide that you have to climb to the top to get on and go down really fast. It was so fun!" Josiah excitedly shared. "Don't tell anybody, but I think daddy was scared. He tried to be brave as he tells me to be, but I think he was scared." Monica laughed in line with her son. Hearing his voice truly warmed her heart. Monica also knew the perceptive five-year-old was right; Casey did not like heights, so she found it a miracle that he even agreed to get on the slide with their son.

Monica listened closely as her son shared his adventures since he had been back in San Diego. It had only been a week since Casey's mom had picked Josiah up to take him back to California for the remainder of the summer. This would be the longest amount of time she's been away from her son. "Baby," Monica interrupted Josiah, "put your daddy back on the phone, I need to speak with him briefly."

"Okay, mommy. Love you!"

"I love you too, JoJo," Monica started, "now go get daddy." Monica gave herself a mental kick for her lapse in word usage. How could she forget "your".

Before Casey dumped her, they lived as a happy family, and Monica would often refer to Casey as daddy when talking to their son. Adjusting to life as a single mother was more difficult than she anticipated. Though in public, Monica was committed to giving the appearance that she was managing her business like a boss bitch, even if on the inside she felt like anything but that.

"Hello?" Casey's deep voice interrupted her thoughts.

"He- hey!" Monica stuttered and recovered, "Hey, yes, so I finally found a school to enroll Josiah in that has an amazing record for Kindergarten that I think he will like."

"Word?" Casey responded giving Monica permission to continue.

"Yes, I'll text you the link to the school so you can look into it for yourself. And it's expensive but not that bad."

"How much is 'not that bad' Monica?"

Monica couldn't figure out why she was nervous as she fidgeted with the pen laying on the notepad next to her, "It's thirty-five thousand a year. But the price does come down each year as long as he stays at the school through the 8th grade," Monica quickly offered for rationale.

"So, what is the preferred tuition payment schedule?" Casey asked, "Do they want monthly payments, or can I just make one payment for the year?"

"The portal allows for us, well you, to determine the fee schedule." Monica started, "I believe the options are month, quarterly or annually. I have a meeting next with the school administrators and will need to provide a five-thousand-dollar deposit to hold JoJo's spot. I should have all of the information then and can send it to you. Do you want me to email it or text it to you?"

"Email it to me. I'll order a cashier's check for the deposit, text me your address and the bank will have it overnighted to you."

"Thank you, Casey."

"You don't have to thank me; Josiah is *my* and I want to make sure he has everything he needs. You're a good mother and I trust your judgment when it comes to our son."

"Thank you," Monica started, "I really appreciate you saying that. There's just one more thing."

"What is that?" Casey asked.

"The school needs to conduct their initial assessment of Josiah before he can officially begin the fall term. And they are expecting to meet him next."

"Monica," Casey started as he pinched the bridge of his nose to alleviate tension, "JoJo is here with me for a limited amount of time. Is there any way they can make an exception to assess him for when he returns after Labor Day? If they need a donation to take this request under consideration let me know."

"I can do that," Monica confirmed.

"Thank you, I really appreciate it."
Monica and Casey remained on the phone a few minutes longer to confirm logistics and to exchange pleasantries before disconnecting the call.

****

"JoJo will be home next weekend, the time flew by," Monica yelled out to her baby sister Sharmaine. "This will be my last weekend free, and I need to enjoy myself before I enter full on mommy and student mode."

Sharmaine was in the full-length hall mirror, adjusting her dress, "I feel you, sis! I am surprised you agreed to come out. You never wanna hang out these days."

"That's because I've been there and done that, plus mothering comes first," Monica said to defend herself.

"Yeah, well, you haven't been out with me." Sharmaine chided as she playfully slapped her sister's butt.

"Hey!" Monica protested, "I'm going to charge you next time you do that."

****

Monica and Sharmaine met up with Sharmaine's friends in the parking lot of Roman's Bar & Lounge to celebrate the birthday of Sharmaine's close friend Tamika. Monica was not wholly comfortable with the group of women because she only knew her sister and Tamika. This would be her first time meeting the other six ladies, and they appeared to be a wild bunch. Monica prayed that the women were not the drama type because she did not have time for any mess.

When the group of women made it to Roman's, Monica watched as her sister walked up to the large, menacing bouncer and hugged him before she motioned for the party to join her at the front of the line. Another bouncer, who looked to be Pacific Islander, emerged from inside the club, smiled at Sharmaine, and proceeded to wave her in. The ladies quickly scampered to catch up to the fast-walking bouncer as he led them deeper inside the establishment.

Roman's was a lot larger on the inside than Monica had anticipated, as the group started to slow down, they were ushered into a roped-off booth on the dance floor just below the elevated stage where the DJ was spinning hot records from the summer. "It's been a while since I've done this," Monica thought.

Monica watched from the safety of their VIP booth as her sister and her friends danced in the middle of the dance floor and only returned for a break or a drink. During this time, Monica had turned down countless offers to dance. She began to tear up as she realized this was the first time she had gone to the club without Casey since college. In the past, she and some of their closest friends would shut the club down. They had done everything from buying the bar to throwing money to dancing on the stage. Now, she sat in the middle of what appeared to be a popular nightclub, sitting alone and looking after shoes and purses.

Monica had been so deep in thought that she had not realized the Music had stopped. "Aye, yo! Are y'all having fun tonight?" The DJ asked the crowd of clubgoers. "I want to bring a man who needs no introduction to the stage." Monica watched as the crowd erupted in cheer. Why were they cheering? The DJ didn't even announce who it was yet, she thought to herself. Monica watched closely to see what was happening on stage but could not get a good angle. The DJ took his place behind the turntables and immediately dropped the beat for one of the summer's musical anthems, and Juve da Great ran onto the stage to perform his hit record. For a moment, Monica found herself stunned. An hour prior, the man rocking the stage had asked her to dance, and she politely declined his offer.

As the music continued and Juve performed his hit records, Monica bopped and sang along to the music. Monica felt a tap on her shoulder and saw it was her sister, motioning for her to join them on the dance floor. Monica obliged her sister's request and quickly wondered where they were going as they walked across the dance floor. At the back of the stage, Monica realized that she and her sister's friend would soon be in the spotlight on the stage with Juve da Great and his Hustle Cru. The music stopped again, and for a moment, she locked eyes with Juve, who had since removed his sunglasses. He winked briefly before turning his attention to Tamika, adorned with her birthday tiara at the center stage. Juve introduced Tamika to the audience and led them as they serenaded her with the Stevie Wonder version of the "Happy Birthday" song.

The ladies remained on stage for one more song as they danced and sang along before they were escorted back to their booth, where they proceeded to party until the club closed at 3 am.

Bailey

"That was an impressive game!" Bailey exclaimed as she and Mike exited Petco Park on a Sunday afternoon.

"Yeah, who would have thought the Padres would be at the top of their division leading into the final months of the baseball season" he responded.

"Exactly!" Bailey continued, "At this time of the year, you hear more about the Giants, Dodgers, or Diamondbacks." Mike nodded affirmingly, "I won't complain. I welcome post-season baseball stress".

Mike found himself intoxicated with Bailey. He had never met a woman who was into sports and still feminine. She was an anomaly, and he wanted more of her. "Hey, let's take a walk around the Gaslamp. Do you have time?" Looking at her watch, Bailey noted it was just past 4 pm.

"Sure, I can hang out a bit longer. I have work in the morning, so I can't stay out too late." Mike looked over at Bailey and smiled with pleasure.

****

Bailey and Mike found their way to the Old Spaghetti Factory, where they dined on classic Italian dishes and had a hearty conversation. Bailey had not realized how much she liked Mike. She knew he was a good guy, but she wasn't sure if he was relationship material. They had spent the entire day together, from catching the daytime Padres baseball game to having dinner. Bailey did not want the day to end.

"So, tell me about your women, Michael?" Bailey asked. Shocked by her question and aroused by how she said his name, Mike choked on his drink of water.

"As you know, I was dating heavy, and things started to get complicated, so I've taken a step back from that life for a while." Bailey was pleased with his response, though she gave him the side-eye because she didn't know how much of that was truth and how much was game. "So, what about you?"

"What about me?" Bailey quizzed.

"Don't play coy." Mike admonished, "How many men are you juggling?"

"I don't juggle men," Bailey laughed out loud, "They simply come and go."

"Damn, it's like that!" Mike said he grabbed his beer, "I'm scared of you."

"Nah, let me stop playing," Bailey started. "I just do me; work, hang out with friends occasionally, and work some more."

"Hmm, I find it hard that a lady such as yourself hasn't been picked up by one of those football players you work with."

"Please," was all Bailey managed to say in response. Mike noticed a slight flinch on Bailey's face after he spoke those words. The movement was so subtle that he would have otherwise missed if he had not studied her all day. More was going on; he knew something would come out if she did not want to fess up now.

"So, Mike," Bailey stated, "We've gone out a few times, and I have enjoyed myself. For some reason today was extra fun. Do you know why?"

Mike noted how Bailey changed the conversation, and while he wanted to know what was going on with her, he followed along with the redirected conversation. "I think because this date was more of a hangout than a 'date-date' which are always weird."

"Agreed," Bailey responded, "I love hanging out with you, you are so funny and have a wealth of information on some of the most random things."

"Yeah, well, you know how I do." Mike started as he dusted off his collar.

"No, I don't," Bailey quipped, "and it is not 2003; please do not dust your shoulders off ever again in life". The two laughed uncontrollably at Bailey's assessment of Mike's actions.

They lingered at the Old Spaghetti Factory for another forty-five minutes before exiting the restaurant and heading to their respective homes to prepare for the work week.

"So, I'll see you Wednesday, yes?" Bailey asked as she was getting into her rideshare.

"Absolutely, gorgeous," Mike replied as he walked toward his condo.

Monica

Monica had spoken to Kenny every day since they met at Roman's two weeks earlier. Kenny, professionally known as Juve da Great, was relentless in his efforts to capture a moment of Monica's time. She had declined his offer to dance and even ignored his invitation to join him in his VIP section, as she had her own with her sister and friends.

Despite Monica's kind denials, Kenny found his opening when the club closed while Monica's group was headed to their cars in a nearby parking lot. The birthday girl, Tamika, stated louder than she would have ordinarily due to inebriation and adjusting to the lack of music that she was hungry. Hearing this, as he was only a few yards away from the ladies, Juve jogged up to the group to persuade them to hang out with him and his guys.

"Aye, we're heading to the Mel's on Parkway if y'all want to get something to eat."

"It's la-," Monica started as she was interrupted by Tamika, "Absolutely! I am starving."

"That would be cool," Monica heard some of the other ladies agreeing. Monica attempted to plea with her sister with her eyes, but it was too late as Sharmaine beamed excitedly. Throwing the subtle approach out the window, Monica contested verbally to sway her sister in her direction. "I'm really tired you guys," Monica started, "I need to get home".

"Awww, come on, Monica," Sharmaine whined. "When was the last time we went out? It's Tamika's golden birthday". Monica sensed all eyes were on her, which caused significant discomfort.

Stalking Monica with his eyes, Juve asked the group of ladies one last time as his homeboys were approaching if they would be joining them at Mel's. "Yes, we'll meet you there," Tamika responded with a hint of annoyance.

****

"You were giving a brother a hard time," Kenny stated with laughter.

"That's because you do not know how to accept 'no' as an answer." Monica continued, "I know you gave your parents a tough time growing up."

"You can say that," Kenny responded, "but I can only be me."

Much to Monica's surprise, Kenny the man was nothing like Juve da Great; Kenny was reserved and laid back, while his rap star alter-ego was high-energy and boisterous.

Going with Kenny and his friends to Mel's after Tamika's party proved to be an adventure Monica was now pleased to have joined. The rowdy group kept the staff of Mel's and other patrons in an uproar despite the time of night – or rather, morning. Monica did not pretend to be surprised when Kenny weaseled his way to sit next to her at the modified elongated table the staff had configured for them in the middle of the restaurant's dining floor.

For the next two hours, Monica, Kenny, and their friends engaged in conversations that ranged from the entertainment industry to their jobs, family, religion, and sports. Kenny had noticed Monica's stoic disposition during that last topic. He wouldn't pry as he did not want to jeopardize his opportunity of getting to know her better. But he promised himself that he would ask about her aversion to professional sports the next time they went out.

Reminiscing on their initial encounter had Monica feeling like a schoolgirl. She shocked herself by her willingness to engage and converse with Kenny. With her breakup from Casey still relatively fresh, Monica did not think she would find another man appealing for months, if not years. Alas, here she was downright smitten with Kenny.

"Well, sir," she started, "I need to get back to my studies."

"See, that's why I like you. I knew you were about something when I laid eyes on you at the club."

"Now, I know you are full of it", Monica replied while chuckling.

"I don't know who hurt you, but you need to learn how to take a compliment." Kenny continued, "I am not one just to blow smoke. Be proud of going back to school. Do you know how many never go back?"

Monica chewed on her bottom lip as she considered Kenny's words. Perhaps she was undermining her abilities, shrinking herself to fit into Casey's world. "Thank you, I appreciate that", she responded earnestly.

"No doubt. I fuck with you, fareal, and I want you to accomplish everything you set your mind out to do."

"Well, that is very sweet of you. I do need to get off this phone, though."

"I gotchu. Before I let you go, are you going out with me on Saturday?" Kenny asked.

"Is this your way of asking me on a date?" Monica quizzed.

"You will know when I am asking you on a date. I want to see you again and have a few things I need to do around the city".

"Boy," Monica started, "you want me to run errands with you?"

Laughing, Kenny answered honestly, "Yeah, something like that, I guess".

"Hmmm, can I let you know tomorrow?" Monica asked.

"Fasho. Don't keep a brother waiting."

"Have yourself a good evening and we will connect tomorrow".

"Later" Kenny offered his standard salutation.

"Later" Monica mimicked.

Bailey

As Bailey opened the bottom right drawer of her cubicle desk, reaching for her purse to prepare for her departure for the day, the desk phone rang. She glanced at the telephone atop her desk and noted it was her boss. "Hey, Johnathan!" Bailey paused as she listened intently to the caller, "Sure, I'll come down now."

Bailey closed her desk drawer and grabbed a pen and notepad as she went to her boss' office. Johnathan sounded uncharacteristically frantic over the phone, which caused Bailey a great deal of concern. Especially since the cause for the call had been the player yearbook, which she had completed a week ago. The only thing she had left to do was the final edits of players who had not made the team, but the production team was managing that part so they could send it to the printer. As far as Bailey was concerned, the project was completed and removed from her plate.

Rounding the corner to Johnathan's office, Bailey noted that the door was closed. He only closed the door if he was on the phone with his wife or if he was in a meeting. Bailey found it odd that Johnathan would take a meeting seconds after he requested to see her. "He could have called me back," she thought as she approached the mahogany door. Bailey rapped lightly on the door as she slowly opened it to peek inside.

"Come in," Johnathan motioned from behind his desk as he abruptly ended his phone conversation. Taking a deep breath, Bailey centered her thoughts on the immediate task before her, walking from the doorway towards the armless chair opposite her boss. To appear confident, Bailey squared her shoulders and looked directly into Johnathan's face instead of searching his desk to see what lay atop it. "Have a seat," Johnathan instructed Bailey.

"Hey, what's up?" Bailey asked her boss, exhausted by the mental games they were engaged in. "You sounded alarmed when you called me, is everything okay?" she asked.

Jonathan riffled through the papers on his desk and responded enthusiastically, "Oh, yes! I did not mean to alarm you." Passing a now organized stack of papers across his desk, Johnathan continued, "The proofs for the players' yearbook came back and I wanted to share them with you."

Pausing momentarily to watch Bailey evaluate the pages, he continued, "The folks upstairs were impressed with the innovative design and layout, and…"

"CONGRATULATIONS!" Bailey heard a chorus ring out behind her. Turning to face the crowd, she was more perplexed now than when she first entered Johnathan's office. She made note that the entire marketing department was quickly filling Johnathan's office: Geneva was holding a cake while Stan was holding a large bouquet of balloons.

"What's going on here?" Bailey asked, puzzled.

"Well," Jonathan started as he rose from his desk chair, "We have been so impressed with you over the last four months that I'd like to offer you a promotion."

Jonathan's words swam around her head in a haze as she processed everything she heard. A promotion? She asked herself. It had only been a few months, and there was no indication that Jonathan was leaning towards bringing her on board as a full-time regular employee. "So…," Johnathan started, interrupting her thoughts, "what say you? Are you going to join the team full-time? We sure would hate to miss keeping a talent like you around long-term".

The last four months rapidly replayed through her mind; the good days outweighed the bad ones. She was sufficiently challenged, had great coworkers, and loved working in professional sports. By her account, understanding how competitive it was to get a job in the American Football League, she would not let this opportunity pass. "Absolutely!" Bailey finally responded to Jonathan's open query.

The marketing team erupted into a louder cheer, welcoming their new permanent coworker. Geneva set the cake she had been holding on Jonathan's desk as he pulled plates and forks from the filing cabinet along the wall of his office door. The team celebrated the occasion with cake and chattering. As Jonathan's office began to quiet with the departure of members of the team heading back to their varied responsibilities, Jonathan began to tidy up his office so that it could be in a condition to work in the following morning. Geneva had the remainder of the cake in her hands to take to kitchen, while Bailey grabbed the balloons to return to her workstation. Before Bailey exited his office,

Jonathan informed her that he would have the offer letter from HR for her to sign in the morning. "Awesome," Bailey responded with glee.

****

Bailey gathered her belongings to leave work for the day, she texted Mike to share her good news. The pair made plans to meet the following day for celebratory drinks. Grabbing the balloons from the corner where she placed them and her purse from its designated location, Bailey exited the building and walked across the parking lot to her vehicle. The late afternoon wind had picked up, creating a challenge for her to place the balloons in the car's trunk. Paying careful attention to not lose or pop a balloon in the process, after a 3-minute battle, Bailey got the trunk to close successfully.

"Happy Birthday, pretty lady," Bailey heard a familiar voice call out.

"It's not my birthday, but thank you," Bailey responded as she turned to face the speaker sitting in his vehicle with the passenger-side window rolled down.

"We've got to stop meeting like this," the speaker chided.

"Or," Bailey paused as she rounded her car for the driver's door, "you can stop following me, Casey."

Casey laughed and began driving away as Bailey entered her vehicle. The hairs at the back of her neck were standing. Why did Casey have such an effect on her? Bailey needed to shake any lingering interests. If for nothing else, she was a professional.

Casey

"All right, little man, I love you." It broke Casey's heart to watch his mother and son enter the San Diego airport for their journey back to Texas. Casey wanted nothing more than to have his son closer to him, to be an everyday parent. It pained him to know that he could not give his son what his father had given him: a stable two-parent home. Casey was not proud of how things went down with Monica, but he needed to breathe; he did not want to feel like a prisoner in a relationship that did not mentally and emotionally stimulate him.

Casey held back tears as he watched his mother guide Josiah through the airport. The regular season started this weekend, and with Monica back in school, Casey had no idea when he would see his son again. He did know one thing; he was blessed to have a supportive mother available to help him be the star in Josiah's eyes.

****

Casey plopped down on the sideline bench, using the towel hanging from the side of his football shorts to wipe away the sweat streaming down his face. The sun was beating on his bare back and chest as the defensive linemen ran drills on the Oilers' practice field. Casey accepted a cup of ice-cold water from a member of the training staff as he sat back to open his lung to suck in more hot air. "Yo! Rook, bring me my bag," Casey demanded of one of the newly drafted players. This was the team's last practice before heading out on Friday to start their season on the road.

The rookie sat Casey's gym bag on the bench beside him as he walked away carrying another player's protective equipment. Casey looked up briefly to watch the young guy walking away, struggling to manage other veteran players' equipment. He smirked and laughed as he remembered his days as a rookie and all of the nonsense he was required to do by the veterans of his time.

Searching an outer compartment of his gym bag, Casey pulled out his cell phone. He checked the activity of missed calls and text messages. He cursed silently when he saw that none of them had been from the one person he was fond of, even after sending her a message that morning. Too tired to lift his head from where he was resting, Casey proceeded to scroll through his social media to get an update on the world outside of football.

"Fuck it!" Casey exclaimed to himself; he completed a few transactions on his phone and rose to leave the practice field for the locker room for a shower and to change. He was more tired than usual, so he scanned the field, looking for a rookie he could order to carry his equipment back to the locker room. Much to his chagrin, there were only veterans, coaches, and members of the training staff left on the field. In a huff, Casey grabbed his gym bag and protective equipment and headed towards the locker room.

Bailey

Bailey was working intently when she was startled by the shrill of her desk phone which abruptly interrupted her workflow. "This is Bailey," she answered while glancing at her phone. She noted that it was just short of 4 pm.

Bailey walked to the reception desk to see what was delivered for her. She did not believe in having personal packages from online shopping stores sent to her job, so the only thing she thought it could be was the annual yearbook. Earlier in the week, the final draft of the yearbook was sent to the printer. And, while the vendor was known to work quickly, a three-day turnaround seemed exceptionally quick. Nevertheless, she proceeded to the reception desk, prepared to ask her colleagues to assist her with hauling the boxes to a more remote location on the office floor.

As she approached the reception desk, Bailey saw that Geneva's face was bright with glee. As Bailey walked closer, she crooked her neck to get a glimpse at what her work friend was gawking at. "Girl, you must have that magic!" Geneva exclaimed as Bailey arrived at the reception desk.

"What are you talk…" Bailey's breath hitched as she saw the elaborate display before her. "Is this for me?" Bailey asked.

"Well, it certainly isn't for me," Geneva teased. "Does your boo have a brother? Because your man, whoever he is," Geneva said, rolling her eyes, "…nose is wide open for you!"

The focal point was an "I miss you" balloon display filled with silver, teal, and black balloons. There were three dozen teal and white roses in a crystal vase, with a card on the vase's side.

Bailey grabbed the card to see who the delivery was from. Deep down, she already knew. The delivery couldn't be from anyone but the gentle giant who wore the number 9-0. She tried to stifle the smile on her face, but the smile in her heart shone brightly through her eyes. "Something tells me you know who sent this." Geneva quizzed.

"Well, if I can get this card open, I'll know for sure," Bailey responded. Was that hope in her voice? She looked around nervously to see if Geneva noticed her eagerness.

Pulling the card from the envelope, Bailey admired the detail of the card's cover. The intricate foil design was marvelous. Gosh, this man leaves no detail undone, she thought to herself. Opening the card, Bailey found a pair of tickets to the Beyoncé concert. She held the tickets up for Geneva to see the card's content. Geneva snatched the tickets from Bailey's hand for further inspection.

"Ummm! These are front-row tickets to Beyoncé!" Geneva's indoor voice shouted.

"I know!" Bailey gushed before going back to the card to read the message.

****

Bailey had much to think about on her drive home that evening. She asked Geneva if she could leave the balloon bouquet at the reception desk, to which Geneva happily agreed, and Bailey took the three dozen roses back to her desk before heading out of the office for the day.

She needed time to think and consider her options and what the immediate and long-term impact would be. Bailey was still dating Mike, who was great but lacked spark in the romance department. Casey, on the other hand, was all spark and no stability. Bailey had never been one to date multiple guys, though, technically, she was not dating Casey. They had gone on a date – yes, but they were not dating. "This is why I like being single," Bailey said aloud to no one.

Bailey did not hesitate to shed her clothes for a hot shower to wash off the day's angst. Standing under the stream of hot water, she allowed it to run down her face while she braced the shower wall. Bailey found resolve in a hot shower whenever life presented uncomfortable circumstances.

And, just like magic, Bailey stepped out of the shower, grabbed her plush red robe from behind the bathroom door, and was ready to solve her problems. Sitting at the foot of her bed, Bailey grabbed her phone that was lying face down on the bedside table. She opened her text messages to send Casey a note of gratitude for his grand gesture and to inform him that she would return the Beyoncé tickets. Soon after pressing send on the message, she blocked Casey's number. Professionalism was important to Bailey, and she could not allow the perception of a romantic relationship to jeopardize everything she had worked for.

Next up on Bailey's agenda was Mike. She needed to give the guy a real chance to see how things could progress. Bailey opted to call Mike instead of sending a text, which was what she originally intended to do. To her surprise, the two held a conversation well past midnight. Before disconnecting for the evening, because they both had work in the morning, Mike made plans to pick Bailey up on Friday for a date.

Don't Tempt Me

Monica

Graduate school was kicking Monica's butt. It had been years since she was a student and setting a study schedule proved to be more challenging than she had imagined, especially now that she was raising Josiah and dating Kenny. She had an ambitious completion schedule and took five courses, the maximum the university would allow. To her benefit, many of her classes were during the day while Josiah was at school. She could drop him off in the morning before going to campus for class or the library.

It was important for Monica not to become distracted by her relationship with Kenny; she had invested everything into her relationship with Casey, which left her a displaced single mother starting over in a new state. She wanted to accomplish something for herself, to be an example to her son. She could not become consumed with Kenny and the benefits of dating Juve da Great.

With focus and dedication, Monica was on track to complete her master's degree in three semesters. And, much to her surprise, Kenny was extremely supportive of her goals. She found he inquired about her studies whenever they spoke and would often cut their phone conversations short to encourage her to study or to spend time with Josiah. Dating Kenny was indeed a breath of fresh air for Monica. He poured into her in ways she didn't even realize she needed. So accustomed to being Casey's plus one and help mate, he rarely affirmed her and expressed his gratitude or appreciation.

Monica wondered how and why she would stay with Casey for so long. The answers to the questions she asked brought tears to her eyes and made her sad. She never thought of herself as someone who would tolerate poor treatment, and yet, because Casey provided a cozy life, she complied with a set of unwritten rules. Rules to a game that had proven to be emotionally damaging. Deep in thought about the last decade of her life, Monica decided to take another step on her journey of liberation. She would look for a therapist to begin unpacking and rebuilding her life from a solid foundation.

****

Monica surprised Josiah with an impromptu visit to San Diego to spend time with his father and to attend an

Oilers game. She was on Fall break and had been in a good place with Casey and felt comfortable with taking the trip for her son. It also did not hurt that things were going extremely well with Kenny. The trip to San Diego would take Monica's mind off the fact that he was on tour and not scheduled to return home to Houston for another two weeks.

Monica knew the risk she was taking with Kenny or better yet, Juve da Great. He had expressed to her early on what his intentions were with her and though he was a platinum selling rapper he had moved on from the party life. In the weeks Monica and Kenny had grown to know one another, she found that he had been a man of his word. Though she had forgiven him, Monica still possessed lingering pain from her relationship with Casey. She vowed to never become engrossed in a man again. The stakes were higher with Kenny as she had her son, Josiah, to consider. Monica had not introduced Kenny to Josiah just yet and with the way things were going between she and Kenny, Monica knew that it was only a matter of time before that would change.

Ziggy Harris

Landing in San Diego was a breath of fresh air for Monica. Growing up in New York City, the California air always felt like a sip of spring water on a hot summer day, crisp and clean. Josiah had fallen asleep on the three-hour plane ride from Houston. Monica carried the not so small boy from the plane up to the terminal gate where she found a vacant seat to sit the child down and wake him. Josiah was slow to break his slumber and whined as his mother ushered him to his feet to begin the trek to baggage claim for their luggage. Smart packing allowed for both Josiah and Monica's shoes, clothing, and toiletries to fit inside of one suitcase. They each had their own backpacks containing personal electronics.

Monica made the short drive from San Diego International Airport to their hotel in the Gaslamp District for an early check-in and to freshen up. Besides the neighborhood being one that Monica really enjoyed, the zoo, museums and other kid-friendly attractions were nearby. Though she anticipated for Josiah to spend as much time with his father as Casey's schedule would allow, she wanted to be sure to fill his time while back in San Diego.

Monica pulled up to Oilers Central in her rented SUV at 12:25pm to reunite with the father of her son. Prior to visiting Oilers Central, Monica took Josiah for his favorite breakfast at the Pancake House. Josiah couldn't resist his favorite Spiderman waffle which was shaped like a spider in a web topped with strawberries and blueberries that had a small Spiderman action figure hanging on the side of the plate.

Monica watched JoJo as he ate his breakfast with one hand and played with his new action figure in the other. Her heart was bursting at the seams with all the love she held for her son. *Ding.* Monica's cell phone notified her of a new incoming message. As much as she wanted it to be Kenny messaging her, she knew it was Casey informing her his practice was over.

Leaving JoJo in his father's care was a much-needed break Monica didn't realize she needed. She was also pleased to find that she no longer harbored ill feelings towards her child's father. Last time Monica had seen Casey she was a scorned woman on a mission. He'd abruptly ended their relationship and had informed her she'd need to move because the house they shared had been sold. Though she felt Casey's approach was rude, Monica was glad to share a child with him. Unlike some other fathers, Casey was engaged as much as his schedule permitted.

Casey

Casey was pleased to find the exchange of JoJo with Monica amicable, pleasant, even. The last time he and Monica had seen one another in person she was demanding and borderline rude. Casey knew it was important to mend their differences so they could be friends and co-parent, but it did not appear to him that that was what she wanted. Perhaps the extra child support payments had eased some of her animosity. Perhaps going back to school served her well and provided inspiration. Either way he was glad she was in good spirits.

Dressed in grey basketball shorts and a sleeveless Oilers hoodie, Casey took Josiah with him into the locker room so he could change into real clothes. Casey set his son up at his locker with his tablet to play kindergarten educational games while he took a shower. He was excited to spend some much-needed time with his favorite guy and welcomed the gleeful nature of his son. Casey had been feeling less than stellar since Bailey declined his grand gesture and returned the VIP Beyoncé tickets. He had women fawning all over him, and yet, had to fall for the one woman who was unimpressed by his stardom.

Returning to his locker to get dressed Casey found a crowd huddled around JoJo, "Aye! What do y'all got going on over there?" he asked as he approached his locker.

"Lil buddy showing us his videos", Trey, the Oilers leading wide receiver answered.

"Videos?" Casey quizzed with amusement on what his son had been up to while in Texas.

"Look, daddy!" Josiah shouted as he turned the tablet to face his father who was still approaching the crowd.

Grabbing the tablet from his son, Casey examined the video that was playing. To his surprise it was a video of Josiah playing tee ball. The kid had a heck of a swing, Casey thought to himself, even for a 5-year-old. A smile crept upon Casey's face as he proudly watched his son hit a "homerun". "Good job champ!" Casey said to his son as he raised his hand for hi-five. Josiah enthusiastically met his father's hand to complete the celebration.

The crowd dispersed, "Come with me, lil' man", Trey instructed Josiah to allow Casey time to get changed.

"Daddy, can I?" Josiah asked, waiting for his father's permission.

"Yeah, go ahead" Casey agreed.

"You know baseball players transition well to wide receivers" Trey teased.

Casey started to respond but looked down to the left of Trey and remembered his son was in the room and shook his head. Casey would remember Trey's little joke and hit him with a stinger at some point in the future during practice. In the world of professional football one can never let a teammate or opponent off the hook.

****

Casey and Josiah walked side by side as they made their way from the locker room through the main floor of the Oilers HQ for the parking lot. "Do you need to go to bathroom JoJo?" Casey asked, stopping short of the exit door at the final bathroom stop before leaving the building.

"Ummm, no." Josiah responded after taking a while to consider the question.

"I think you should try before we leave, we have a long drive." Casey said trying to cajole his son into taking a bathroom break.

"No, I'm fine" Josiah said attempting to reassure his father, "I am a big boy."

"Okay, well, I want you to go to the bathroom." Casey said as he grabbed his son's hand and led him in the direction of the men's room.

Feeling defeated, Josiah protested "I can go by myself."

The young boy walked slowly to the open entrance of the bathroom against his own desire. Casey waited patiently against the wall for his son to return. For someone who didn't need to use the restroom Josiah took a long time, Casey thought to himself.

Shifting his weight while leaning against the wall Casey's line of vision went from the parking lot exit doors to the main lobby of the Oilers headquarters. The middle elevator opened and let out the passengers that were riding in the car. Casey immediately stiffened to stand straight up supported by his weight alone. He felt the air getting tight in an open walkway. It had been weeks since he last seen Bailey and she was just as beautiful as he remembered her.

She is so beautiful, I bet she hasn't thought a lick about me Casey thought to himself. Well, maybe she does feel something for me Casey thought as he witnessed a slight stutter in Bailey's stride as she approached the direction of the parking lot exit. Casey could feel the electricity between them as Bailey drew nearer. Perhaps he still had a chance with the woman of his waking dreams. Unsure of how to play the situation Casey decided to take a chance. "Hey Ms. Bailey", he said when she was about two steps up from where he stood.

"Hello Mr. Christopher" Bailey responded. She went professional Casey thought to himself, "How are you on this beautiful day?"

"I am well, thank you for asking. How about yourself?" Bailey asked while slowing her stride to half pace.

She's slowing down, great; now all I need is for her to stop, Casey thought to himself. "Well," Casey started…

"I'm ready to go daddy!" JoJo mumbled as he hurried out of the men's restroom.

Casey took note of Bailey's face when she asked, "Who is this?"

"I'm JoJo" the enthusiastic boy responded beaming at Bailey.

"This is my son Josiah. He just got into town." Casey shifted his vision from Bailey to his son, "Did you wash your hands?"

"Dad," Josiah groaned, "yes", he responded, raising his hands for his father to inspect.

"Well, it was nice to meet you Josiah" Bailey said as she reached into her oversized shoulder bag. "Mini football?" she asked.

"Yes!" Josiah exclaimed and grabbed the football from Bailey's hand. "I like her daddy. She's nice and pretty" JoJo continued.

Blushing, Bailey brushed her hair behind her ears. "I have to get out of here, but you two enjoy your day."

"We're heading out ourselves, we can walk out with you." Bailey shifted her weight back to her heels. Sensing her discomfort Casey followed-up "That is if you don't mind."

Looking around "Sure," she hesitated.

Under normal circumstances Casey would not have imposed his will on a woman who was visibly uncomfortable by his presence. This, however, was different. He yearned for Bailey and if an awkward walk to the parking lot was all he had then he would take full advantage of the opportunity.

"Well, I am this way," Bailey said, pointing left when they made it to the edge of the parking lot.

"I'm parked in the other direction," Casey shared, but Josiah and I will walk you to your car.

"No, really, that's unnecessary," Bailey complained.

"Well, you know I'm a true gentleman and I have to teach the young one…" Casey said, winking at Josiah, "…how to treat a lady."

Looking down at the sweet face of the young boy, she agreed to allow him and his father to escort her to her vehicle. Bailey parked in the third aisle from the far end of the parking lot in the middle of the section. Approaching her bright red car, Bailey thanked Casey and Josiah for seeing her safely to her vehicle. "You are the perfect little gentleman," she said, looking down at Josiah.

"Daddy, where are we going? Can Ms. Bailey come with us?"

Shocked by his innocent question, Bailey quickly interrupted before any more bright ideas could be shared out loud.

"Oh, sweetie, I am still working. I must get across town for a meeting," Bailey said, letting the boy down gently.

"Okay," Josiah said somberly. "Maybe next time".

"Yes, maybe next time," Casey said as he grabbed his son's hand.

Bailey could not send the adorable cherub away sad, "You two have a good day, and I look forward to hearing all about your adventure." She prayed that a sliver of hope would cheer him up.

It worked, Bailey thought when Josiah said, "Okay!"

Don't Tempt Me

Bailey

The warm leather seats comforted Bailey's back and buttocks as she settled into the driver's seat of her red Dodge Charger. She unexpectedly ran into Casey and his adorable son while leaving the office for a late afternoon meeting. She found the little boy to be just as energetic as his father. At only four- or five-year-olds, Bailey concluded the magnetic boy would give his mother a run for her money in about ten years. Casey was a ladies' man, and the apple did not fall far from the tree.

Bailey had a quick drive to the local youth organization that was scheduled to be recognized during a home game opening ceremony. Youth Fusion would receive a $10,000 grant and 50 tickets for students, staff, and parents to attend the game. She needed to meet with the Executive Director to collect information on the organization to be used in the game day program. While she could have requested the information via email, Bailey found it more impactful to visit the organizations personally. She could write a more authentic story and take her own photos.

141

Ziggy Harris

****

Happy hour any day of the week, had become Bailey's favorite after-work activity. If she wasn't meeting with Sierra, then it would be Mike. Tonight, the foursome; Bailey, Mike, Sierra and Corey would be gathering for a double date. Bailey had initially made plans for she and Mike for Thursday at Lady Isabel's in La Jolla, but Sierra had called her that morning asking if they could meet for drinks after work. Bailey had done her best to explain that she already had plans with Mike, which Sierra found was an excellent opportunity for all the friends to gather.

Bailey met Mike at his apartment so he could make the short drive north to meet their friends. The evening breeze washed Bailey's face as she rested her head on the headrest with the window down, watching traffic. Driving was Bailey's place of comfort when needing to think. But riding and watching was her preferred place of peace. She observed the sights and sounds of the roadways and highways. Being with Mike felt right, and it made sense, she thought to herself. Yet, while sitting comfortably next to Mike and thinking about all the peace and happiness he added to her life, Bailey's mind drifted to Casey. Casey represented chaos and confusion, but she was drawn to him. Frustrated by her thoughts deceiving her, she forced herself to think about something other than Casey.

Bailey reached for Mike's right hand resting on the center console; she slipped her left-hand, palm side up, underneath his, giving a light squeeze. Mike responded to Bailey's affection with a soft smile; she felt reassured that Mike was where she needed to be. "What do you think Sierra and Corey want to share with us?" Bailey asked, interrupting the silence.

"Well," Mike began, "it can only be one of two things. They are either engaged or having a baby".

"Babies are nice, but I prefer a wedding over a baby shower. I love dressing up!" Bailey shared exuberantly.

"Yeah, I tend to look good in a penguin suit," Mike snickered.

"As fine as you are, I'm sure you would be hella cute in a penguin suit and bowtie!" Bailey said as she brushed the side of his face with the back of her hand.

Mike opened his mouth to respond, then shut it as he found himself without a suitable response he felt comfortable sharing out loud.

Monica

Driving through her old neighborhood, Monica was surprised that she felt nothing. She hadn't realized how suffocated she had been in Casey's world and how being with him stifled who she was. Monica committed herself while she was waiting at a red light, not to allow herself to get consumed by Juve's life. The newfound freedom was refreshing.

There was no more space in Monica's life to re-live the past. There were good times, and there were terrible times. For now, she was committed to the present and managing how to start her legal career. Thankfully, she and Casey had agreed to a fair amount of child support. While her life would be less glamorous in Houston than in San Diego, she would not be down in the dumps. Not needing to work a nine-to-five while in school was very helpful. She would continue taking courses during the day and could explore internship opportunities. Life was good, and Monica wanted to enjoy every bit of it. Her son adored her, she was working towards her professional goals, and the blossoming relationship with Kenny fed her soul. Her thoughts were suddenly interrupted by the shrill of her ringing phone. Picking the phone up to glance at the screen to see who the caller was, a smile crept across Monica's face.

"Hello," she answered while pressing the speaker button and placing the phone back into its original position in the cup holder.

"What's going on beautiful?"

Monica loved that Kenny showered her with compliments, although they often made her uncomfortable. She wasn't used to a man consistently pouring into her with goodness. Casey wasn't mean to her per se; he just took her for granted. Despite her conflict with receiving compliments, she vowed never to complain because receiving them was much better than not receiving them.

"I dropped JoJo off with his father earlier, and now I'm driving around trying to decide what to do next. Being in San Diego is so weird now that my life is in Texas. I thought about going to some of my old hangout spots, but honestly, I don't want to see any of those people," she responded.

"How about you pick me up this evening and we can make some new memories in San Diego?"

"What are you talking about, Kenny?" Monica asked.

"My shows in Denver are postponed because something happened at the arena. I don't know what, but my road manager told me they had to cancel my shows for tomorrow and the next day," he replied.

"Wow! That is crazy," Monica responded in disbelief.

"The crew is heading to Seattle, and I was going to head down to you. If that was cool with you." Kenny quizzed.

"You know what," Monica paused, "I would love that! What time does your flight land?"

"Seven, but I'll text you the flight information," Kenny shared. Monica and Kenny shared their final pleasantries before ending the call.

Bailey

"Can you believe it?" Bailey gushed over the phone. She and Mike recapped the previous night's event as she finished preparing for work.

"Yeah, man. Those two are taking a huge step," Mike responded.

"I mean that was a huge announcement. I mean, I'm happy for them, but I don't know," Bailey sighed.

"They are adults, and this is their decision," Mike admonished Bailey, "you can be a friend and support them or not".

Mike's brute response took Bailey aback. She had never heard him take such a tone in all the time they had spent together. She wondered why he just didn't say he disagreed with her. Unsure of how to proceed, she decided to end the conversation. "I hear you; buying a home with someone you're not married to can be a liability." Bailey glanced at the clock on her nightstand, "have you made it to work yet?"

"I'm about five minutes away. I made you mad, and you want to rush me off the phone now?" Mike teased.

"No," Bailey lied. "I'm running late, and I need to get a move on it."

"Fa sho. Hit me up when you get settled at work," he replied.

****

Work came as a welcomed distraction. As much as she wanted to shake the feeling, Bailey found her spirit conflicted by her interaction with Mike that morning. She could not discern if she felt Mike was chastising her like a child or whether he was trying to invalidate her opinions. Either way, she was not pleased with their conversation and needed to figure out how or if she should address it.

It was nearing the end of the day before Bailey realized she had not eaten anything. She opened her bottom left drawer and grabbed a granola bar. Taking advantage of the mini break she gave herself, she fished for her phone in the sweater pocket she had left it in when she arrived at work. Inspecting the damage from intentionally ignoring her phone, Bailey found the damage was quite minimal. A few missed calls and a handful of text messages. She made a mental note to return Sierra's missed call while driving home. There were texts from her father, Mina, and Mike. Bailey quickly responded to her dad and Mina's messages. She paused to read the texts she had received from Mike. Checking the timestamp, he'd been trying to contact her for most of the day. To ease his mind, Bailey found the message she would respond to. "I'm good, busy day" was all she managed responding to Mike's message asking if she was okay.

The last few hours of work breezed by. Bailey ordered Italian for pickup and would have a Lisa Vanderpump-approved glass of wine when she got home. Though work was routine and uneventful – for which she was delighted – Bailey remained uneasy about Mike. It was far too early in their situation to be experiencing these types of issues. Bailey's father never silenced her or made her feel like her opinions were insignificant, no matter how outrageous they were. From childhood, she was given the space to express herself fully and expected that to continue with her adult relationships. Perhaps she was being too hard on Mike, Bailey wondered. She would use the evening to process her feelings about Mike and if she wanted to move forward.

As she exited the Oilers executive offices, Bailey paused; she was in shock when she saw Mike standing by her car holding flowers. She was parked in the aisle aligned with the doors several rows back. However, even from a distance, she could see her car and who was standing near it. She didn't know if she was shocked or upset that he would come to her job unannounced. Bailey always tried to separate her personal and professional life, and Mike showing up at her job was a much more egregious offense than his unpleasant remarks this morning.

Bailey hated being fake and putting on false airs, but she had no choice if she didn't want to cause a scene outside of her workplace. She gathered her composure and pushed through the double doors towards the parking lot. The light breeze brushed across her face as she inhaled. Countless scenarios played in her mind as she walked through the parking lot. Bailey was pleased to find the parking lot was virtually empty; few cars in the parking lot meant few people were in the building. She hoped she could settle things with Mike quickly and not be seen.

Bailey reassured herself that she could handle the situation before her swiftly and tactfully, and heaven help her, unnoticed by colleagues.

Bailey noticed Mike stiffened his back as she approached him. The flowers he held, a vibrant arrangement of orange lilies, sunflowers, yellow roses, and crimson daisies, were stunning. She consciously tried to maintain a deadpan expression; Friday family poker night served her well, especially for moments like this. Mike broke into a nervous smile when Bailey finally reached him.

He left work early to check on Bailey because he had sensed something was wrong, though he could not identify what it could be. They had a great double date last night in La Jolla with Sierra and Corey and even had their daily morning conversation. Bailey had rushed him off the phone, but he figured it was because she was running late. Her significantly delayed and short message left him confused. Mike acted swiftly to address whatever grieved her right away, even if that meant showing up to her job and potentially looking like a fool. She was exceptional, and Mike wanted Bailey to know that. So, he forwarded all his calls to his mobile phone, found a florist, and sprang into action.

"Nice flowers," Bailey said when she finally reached Mike.

"I am glad you like them," he responded, handing Bailey the grand bouquet in a red vase.

Bailey accepted the arrangement without hesitation, "What are you doing here?" she asked.

"You seemed upset with me, so I came to check on you," Mike paused, "I know you're wondering why I'm at your job, but I needed to see you right away," he explained.

"Wow" was all Bailey's brain could get her mouth to agree to. This man left work early to check on her, a lovely and noble gesture Bailey assessed internally. "I ordered takeout then heading home. Would you like to go with me to Luigi's and have our conversation there?" Bailey wanted to talk with Mike, just not in the parking lot at her job.

"It's Thursday night, and that place is going to be busy. Would it be possible if we updated the order and went to either your place or my house?" Mike asked.

Bailey was preparing to respond when she was interrupted by the loud bass of a car passing by. Her back had been to the building, so she could not see who had entered the parking lot. The music became louder, indicating that someone was driving in their direction. It was a Friday afternoon, and people should be leaving the stadium, not coming to it. Bailey began to pray profusely. Slowly turning to her right, a sizeable blacked-out F-150 pickup truck stopped.

"Shit!" Bailey whispered. God did not receive her prayers early enough to intervene.
The driver of the oversized pick-up truck slowly rolled down his deep-tinted window. "Hey Ms. Bailey", he said.

Shifting her weight to steady her composure, Bailey adjusted the flowers she held, "Hello Mr. Christopher." She debated whether to introduce Mike and cursed Mike inside her head for appearing unannounced at her job.

Casey's arrogance decided for her, "Hey man," he started.

"Mike. His name is Mike." Bailey reluctantly made the introduction. "Mike, this is Casey Christopher and Casey, this is Mike."

"Aye man, nice to meet you", Mike chirped as he walked to Casey's vehicle to shake his hand.

"Fa sho," Casey responded. "Did Ms. Bailey take you on a tour of our palatial palace?"

"Not yet" Mike stated, "I stopped by to surprise her." Bailey watched the volleying between the two men uncomfortably as they exchanged a relatively pleasant conversation as they jockeyed for a permanent position in her life.

"Mike and I have to get going," Bailey announced as she interrupted the two men's conversation.

"Say, man, have a good game this weekend," Mike offered.

"Thanks. Y'all be easy," Casey said as he rolled up his window and rode away.

Turning her attention from the departing vehicle, Bailey recomposed herself, "I already have an order started at Luigi's. I'll go pick it up and can meet you at your place."

"Sounds good", Mike agreed.

Casey

Seeing Bailey in the parking lot with another man was the last thing Casey expected when he left the facility for the day. Whoever Mike was, Casey thought it must be serious between he and Bailey if he showed up to her job, with flowers no less. He needed to clear his head and tone down the frustration he felt. Casey turned up the music on the radio and drove home. Lucky for him, his son and mother were in town and would be at his house when he arrived, those two were instant mood enhancers. If anyone could brighten his day, it's undoubtedly his son JoJo.

The demands of being a professional athlete were taxing during the season and were much more complicated when having his son in town. Casey was ever so grateful his mother was willing and able to support him when he had Josiah. Otherwise, it wouldn't be possible. Thinking about the unconditional love he receives from his mom, Casey stopped to pick something up for her to express his gratitude. Janette didn't like her son to make a big fuss over her, so he decided to keep his token of appreciation small.

* * * * * * * * * * * * * * * * * * * *

Casey was greeted with the aromatic scents of
vanilla, cinnamon, and sugar as he walked through the
doors of his Chula Vista home. A smile warmed his heart
as he inhaled the sweet smell of what he hoped would be a
cake or a pie. Looking down at the flowers in his hands,
Casey was grateful he had the mind to pick something up
for his mother.

"I am going to get fat!" Casey said to his mom as he
entered the kitchen.

"Are these for me?" Janette exclaimed as she took
sight of the ornate floral arrangement.

"Who else are they gonna be for?" Casey teased as
he handed his mother the flowers and went to the oven to
identify the source of his newly awakened sweet tooth.
Cracking open the oven door for a peek, Casey sprang up in
excitement. "Cookies!" he exclaimed.

"Boy! Get out of the oven." Janette said as she
shooed her youngest son away from the oven. "The first
batch of cookies are in that container over on the island."
Janette started as she pointed in the direction of the

cookies. "You would have seen them if you weren't in my business she teased.

Casey strolled over to the island placed in the middle of his large eat-in kitchen and reached for the rectangular container. From the side, he could feel the warmth of the contents. He placed his hands on either side of the container to allow the warmth to permeate his body. "It's quiet in here ma. Where is JoJo?"

"He's in his room napping. That child has a lot of energy, and I let him run it out," Janette responded as she handed her son a glass of water.

"Oh, so you let him do whatever he wants, hunh?" Casey asked.

"Well, he's a little boy and little boys need space to release their energy." She replied.

"Yeah, okay." Casey retorted, "If it was me, you'd have me on the couch reading a book."

"Hush ya mouth. I let you outside to play." Janette defended herself as she swiped at her youngest son with the kitchen hand towel.

"Since you been baking up a storm, where do you want to go for dinner tonight?"

"Flowers and dinner?" Janette questioned, "What's going on with you?"

"Nothing", Casey lied. "I just wanted to show you some appreciation. Today is my last day being available and you all are leaving on Monday."

"I see," Janette eyed him suspiciously. "You're starting to miss your family?"

"Sorta. In a way." Casey responded honestly.

"Have you spoken to Monica? Are you beginning to regret your decision about ending things with her?" His mother asked.

"Oh nah, definitely not." Casey started. "I miss my son and it bothers me she took him halfway across the country. I don't know why she couldn't stay here in San Diego."

Sighing, Casey's mother responded, "Boy, sometimes I wonder who raised you. No son of mine would be so inconsiderate."

Janette raised her hand to silence her child's objection.

"That girl moved across the country for you. San Diego is not her home so why in the good Lord's name would she stay here? Her family and support system is somewhere else. On top of all of that, you broke her heart!"

"Y'all women always sticking together. I'm your child." Casey complained.

"Monica is the mother of my grandchild. If she is not mistreating that baby upstairs, then she has the right to make the best decisions for herself and him, something you, my darling cherub, did not do." Janette chastised.

"Alright, Mom," Casey said as he stretched, "I'm going to shower. We can go to Bistecca once Jo wakes up."

"Okay, baby," Janette said, handing her son another cookie before he exited the kitchen.

Monica

Monica was smitten with Kenny. He had utterly swept her off of her feet when he made a detour from his tour schedule to San Diego. Kenny was on the west coast and had a few concert dates rescheduled, and he opted to make the short trip to San Diego versus heading to the next city and hanging with his road team.

When Monica picked Kenny up from the San Diego airport, he greeted her with a single rose and a large gift bag. She excitedly hugged Kenny around his neck, dwarfing Monica at 5 feet six inches with his six-foot four-inch frame; Kenny leaned down to embrace the exchange fully.

Breaking from the hug and stepping back, Monica reached for the rose and the bag, "Ah! Not yet", Kenny teased as he held the rose out to Monica and the large bag back from her.

"What do you mean?" Monica whined. "You can't have a big ole gift bag for me and then withhold it. That's not fair!"

"Trust me, you don't want to be in an airport baggage claim when you open this up, Shorty," Kenny reassured as he leaned in to kiss Monica on her forehead.

"Sure." Monica responded, rolling her eyes, "So where do you want to go first?"

"This is your old stomping ground, you tell me." Kenny said, grabbing Monica's hand to lead her out of the airport.

****

"The beach is always so peaceful. You don't get this type of view being in New York. I love home, but this, this is life. The fresh air. The sand. The clear water! It really doesn't get much better than this." Monica mused while standing at the lip of the Pacific Ocean.

"This *is* nice." Kenny agreed. "Cali has some nice beaches."

Monica and Kenny stood on the edge of the beach with their toes buried in the sand until the sun set. "Well, it's about that time we head out," Kenny said, interrupting the silence.

Looking up at the man who brought so much light into her life, Monica smiled at him sweetly and said, "Well, let's get a move on it. I'm hungry. Are you hungry?"

"Famished," Kenny responded.

"Perfect!" Monica exclaimed. "There's a new steakhouse near my hotel. Will that work for you?"

"You know I'm a country boy." Kenny replied, laughing.

****

Monica parked the rented SUV across the street from Bistecca, the new steakhouse she told Kenny about when they were leaving Mission Beach. He grabbed the large bag from the vehicle's trunk and held Monica's hand as he led her to the restaurant's entrance.

Monica and Kenny were greeted by a charty maître d', who had done their best to maintain professionalism once they recognized who was standing in the restaurant's foyer. Kenny continued to be humbled when a fan recognized who he was while out doing ordinary things. The maître d' escorted he and Monica to a remote part of the restaurant where they could have privacy and minimal interruption.

Monica was a veteran of dating men in the spotlight, so she was well-versed in managing fans' excitement and being interrupted while out in public. What was different for Monica was how Kenny or Juve da Great managed fans differently from Casey. Casey maintained his boundaries and did not engage with fans often when he was having "family time" or "date night." On the other hand, Kenny was committed to upholding his Juve persona and giving his fans a show. So, she was aware when she needed to adjust to the interruptions during date night to become a semi-professional photographer for exuberant fans who wanted to capture the moment.

Settling into a corner booth, Monica redirected her focus to the large gift bag Kenny placed between them. "Now, can I see what's in the bag?" Monica asked with feigned annoyance.

"Go right ahead, Shorty, it's all yours," Kenny boasted.

Placing the large, decorated bag on the table, Monica eagerly removed tissue paper from the top and began to pull out boxes. Four to be exact. The boxes varied in size from medium to small. Monica estimated that the two smaller boxes were jewelry, perhaps earrings and a necklace. The larger boxes were a mystery, so she decided to open those last.

Opening the rectangular box first, Monica found a red box, "Cartier?" she asked with a Texas-wide grin. Kenny offered a smile and a nod as his response. Pressing the tiny latch on the box, Monica flipped the lid to absorb the bling before her eyes. Diamond studs sat proudly against the black velvet interior of the box. Monica calculated they were at least three carats of the highest-grade diamonds. The clarity was immaculate. "These are gorgeous," Monica gushed as she leaned over to kiss Kenny. "I don't even know what to expect in the rest of these boxes," she shared excitedly.

"I'm glad you like them." Kenny winked and offered a sly grin.

Monica closed the box of earrings, sat them on the table, and picked up the square box. She removed another red jewelry box. Taking the same action she had done to open the first box; Monica opened the second box; inside she found a bangle bracelet in the form of a cheetah. She lifted the bracelet from its cradle and held it between her thumb and forefinger to examine it further. "This is nice," Monica purred in admiration.

The third box, more significant in size than the first two, contained a trio of Tom Ford private blend parfums. Monica lifted each bottle from their resting place individually to take in their fragrance. "These are amazing! Let me find out you know how to pick perfumes", Monica exclaimed.

"Well..." Kenny chuckled, "You know how I do."

"Yeah, okay," Monica replied, giving Kenny a side-eye. "So far, so good. I can't wait to see what's in box number four." She removed the top of the fourth and largest box and pulled out a grey Ferragamo top-handle cross-body purse. "Sir!" Monica exclaimed as she closely examined the bag's exterior and interior. "Honestly," Monica started as she laid the bag back in the box, "These are some nice gifts. Thank you for thinking about me."

"Anything for you, Shorty," Kenny reassured. "I enjoy making you smile, and if you let me, I'll commit the rest of my life to making you happy."

There was comfort in Kenny's words. However, Monica needed to determine if she and Kenny were ready to discuss a long-term commitment. Casey never wanted to talk about the future, and now she had a man who has been planning a future with her from the moment they met, and Monica now felt unsure of herself. Shifting in her seat, Monica craned her neck to show the man who showered her with love that she appreciated him by placing a soft kiss to his cheek.

The waiter took their cue to approach Monica and Kenny for their orders when Monica removed the boxes and bag from the table. They had not yet to had the opportunity to look at the menu due to the spectacle of gift opening, so Kenny made a generic order of surf and turf with a loaded baked potato and broccoli. Monica settled quickly on filet mignon with mashed potatoes and asparagus.

In an extreme public display of affection, the two chatted in their booth holding hands and making love to each other with their eyes while waiting for their meal to arrive. Monica turned her attention from Kenny when she felt the energy of the waiter approaching them. Taking a beat to focus her gaze, Monica realized that it was not the waiter bringing their meal. A fan, perhaps, she thought. That is until she could make out the figure who was but a few strides away from their table. Adjusting uncomfortably in her seat, Monica stiffened her back and prepared for an uncomfortable conversation.

"Monica…" The deep voice said, "I thought I saw you over here."

"Hi Casey." Monica paused, "This is Kenny." Turning from Casey to Kenny, she completed the introduction, "Kenny, this is Casey."

"What's up, man?" Kenny asked, outstretching his hand towards Casey.

"What's up…" Casey greeted the man who was cozying up to the mother of his child and completed the handshake. "Aye…" Casey began with a hint of confusion, "aren't you the rapper, Juve?"

"Why, yes, I am," Kenny replied, "…and you are Casey Christopher of the San Diego Oilers."

"Well…" Monica interrupted the testosterone fueled battle, "Now that we have made our introductions, Kenny, as you know, Casey is my ex and Josiah's father."

"Well, aren't I at a disadvantage here? Juve knows all about my family and me, and I don't know a thing about him," Casey pouted.

"Casey, you are not entitled to know what goes on in my personal life. We talk about our son and that's it."

"Say, man, I know this might feel weird for you because this is certainly unexpected for me. I'm in town until Saturday morning. How about we go have a beer and talk mano y mano?" Kenny offered.

"I'm not available this weekend but get my number from Monica and give me a call," Casey replied. "I didn't mean to interrupt what you all got going on. Have a good evening. Monica, I'll be seeing you. And Juve, I'm holding you to that call."

Before Casey turned away, Monica could see that he was hurt. "Well," Monica started, "that was awkward and could have gone off the rails. Thank you so much for being cool." Leaning in for a kiss, Monica continued, "If I haven't told you before, I really do appreciate you."

Bailey

Bailey spent the last three days with Mike at his home after he popped up at her job for a surprise apology. She found the uninterrupted time together well spent. They cooked together, binge-watched television, went on hikes, and vegged out around the house. For the first time in their relationship, Bailey felt relaxed; she was able to be a more authentic version of herself.

While she certainly appreciated the time she and Mike spent together, initially, Bailey was hesitant. Mike convinced Bailey to play hooky from work on Friday and spend the day with him. After much persuasion, Bailey eventually obliged Mike's many pleas. When Saturday afternoon arrived, Bailey informed Mike that she would be heading home as she was wearing the clothes from her emergency bag and desperately needed to change. Springing into action, Mike drummed up alternative solutions for Bailey's clothing problem. Bailey agreed to allow Mike to drive her home so she could pack a bag, which included work clothes for Monday, *"just in case."*

Much to Bailey's surprise, settling her differences with Mike was more amenable than she had imagined. Contrary to her initial belief, Mike wanted to hear what Bailey had to say and apologized for his previous tone with her. Mike explained that he wanted to avoid getting too wrapped up in their friend's relationship and would always take a supportive approach to Corey and Sierra. Bailey respected Mike's position and agreed they should not discuss their friends' lives in detail if it were best for their relationship. Though the initial conversation felt heavy, Bailey was glad they had it, and it felt like a weight was lifted off her chest. She committed herself to being present and taking more time to learn Mike.

****

"What do you have planned this week?" Mike asked as he returned to the living room, handing Bailey a glass of water.

"Just the same ole rodeo," Bailey started, "I need to complete a project, and I hope these guys win so everyone will be in a good mood when I reach out to them," she concluded, pointing at the television where the Oilers were playing the New York Islanders.

"So, if I wanted to take you out on a date Wednesday, you'd be available?" Mike asked.

Taking a moment to run her evening agenda through her mental calendar, Bailey had only planned to meet Sierra for happy hour on Friday, which she would not cancel, seeing that she canceled this week's standing social date. "Yes," Bailey hesitated, "I can be available for a date on Wednesday. What did you have in mind?"

"This week is the annual industry conference, and my company is hosting it this year. Wednesday night is the gala, and I would love for you to accompany me," Mike shared.

"Wow…" a perplexed Bailey responded.

Sensing Bailey's ambivalence, Mike reassured her unspoken concerns, "Honestly, I wouldn't be going if we were not hosting. I need to go, make an appearance, and then leave." Bailey nodded as she weighed the information Mike shared. "We can go late and leave early," he offered.

"I'll need to get something to wear," Bailey paused, "…but, I'll go. We don't have to leave early. If I'm going to get all gussied up, then I need to make sure the people see me".

Mike reached over to Bailey to wrap her in a secure embrace. "Thank you," he said as he placed a gentle kiss on the top of her forehead.

Casey

"Outside of you and Jo being here, this past week has been awful," Casey complained to his mother as he chauffeured her and Josiah to the San Diego airport. His mother and son would meet Monica for a flight back to Texas.

"I know you guys lost yesterday, but you already know how the game goes," Janette responded.

Glancing at his son in a booster seat in the back of the pickup truck, Casey wanted to confirm if his son had his headphones on before continuing. "I'm not worried about the game, though losing didn't help," Casey shared.

"Then what is it?" Janette asked. "You've been in a mood since last Thursday." She continued.

Tightening his grip on the steering wheel, Casey grappled with the tiny voice in his head and his feelings, unsure if he should come clean to his mother about his sour mood. "It's Bailey," Casey exclaimed.

"Son? Who is Bailey?" Janette quizzed.

"Bailey is one of the suits in the organization that I was courting and who abruptly ended things," Casey shared. "We had a really nice date, and she acted like she was into me. Then, the other day, he continued, she was in the parking lot with her boyfriend".

"You were courting a young woman at your job? What did she say when she broke it off?" Janette asked.

"I don't know," Casey paused, "…something about maintaining professional boundaries and integrity."

"That sounds reasonable, Casey. It seems like she doesn't want to compromise her career." Janette offered. "Have you ever considered how dating you may have a negative impact on her success?" Jeanette asked.

"No. Not really", Casey responded, "I'm used to women being available for me. Mom, I know that's not what you want to hear but it's the truth. So how do I get Bailey to come to my side and see things my way?"

"Well…" Jeanette paused. "It's not always about you. Perhaps if you took a moment to appreciate and respect the fact that this young woman has a career of her own, then you'd see that it's not about her coming to your side but about you meeting her somewhere in the middle," Jeanette concluded.

"I'm really not trying to hear all that. I'm a star. Who wouldn't want to be with a star?" Casey boasted.

"Boy! If you weren't driving, I'd go upside your head with my purse. I don't know who the hell you think you are, Casey Jeremiah Christopher, but don't be so proud where you believe the world owes you something, because it doesn't. You may be high on the hog now, but when this all goes away who and where will you be?"

"Mom…"

"Don't interrupt me," Janette commanded as she pointed her index finger. "Let me ask you when you decided to…" Janette looked in the back seat to check on her grandson, "leave Monica," she whispered, "What was the reason?"

Massaging his neck with his right hand, "She lost her ambition, her drive for life. I felt like she retired," he answered reluctantly.

"That's exactly what you told me, and now you are moping around because the woman you like, whether she likes you or not, has decided not to pursue a relationship with you because let me get this straight," Janette mocked, "Because of her career."

"Well, when you say it like that" Casey grumbled.

"Say it like what? I'm going off the information you just told me. Listen, baby, the world does not revolve around you. Bailey's world does not revolve around you. Either you want a working woman, or you don't, but you absolutely cannot have it both ways", Janette reassured. "You need to figure it out soon. You're almost 30, and I want some more grandbabies from you," she said while popping him on the arm.

"I hear you. Did you know that Monica has a new boyfriend!" he announced.

"Yes, she is seeing someone new. I am aware." Janette responded casually.

"Why didn't you tell me?" Casey demanded.

"Because that is not my business. I knew when she was ready to tell you, she would." Janette reassured her ailing son.

"Well, she didn't tell me. I spotted her and that rapper guy in Bistecca last week." Casey shared.

"Is that why you rushed out of there after you came back from the restroom?" Janette asked.

"Yeah," Casey admitted.

"Child, I don't know what I'm going to do with you!" Janette started, "You have been around here like a sad puppy because the woman you left and the woman you want are enjoying their lives? If I didn't know you were your father's son, I know now. You cannot be upset at the world because people are moving on in their lives. Be happy for them and wish them well. You and Monica are in a good place, don't ruin it with jealousy."

"I'm not…" Casey started.

"Yes, you are. You thought that woman would be begging to get back with you or sitting home lonely. She's young, and since you didn't want her, let her have a chance at love with someone who does. Plus, from what I hear, Kenny is a kind young man who treats her better than some people I know." Janette shared.

"Wow! You are throwing daggers at me, and I am your child." Casey feigned hurt.

"Well, baby, the truth is the truth."

"I love you, Mom, and I really appreciate you. You make life easier," Casey said as he parked the SUV along the curb at the airport departure terminal gates. He grabbed his mother and son's bag from the vehicle's trunk and carried them to the curb. When Janette freed Josiah from his booster seat, Casey hugged his son tightly while his mother organized her personal belongings and their luggage.

"I love you, son," Casey shared as he squeezed JoJo tight in a hug.

"Don't cry dad. I'll be back", the young boy said, reassuring his father.

"Look out for your grandma and your mother," Casey encouraged.

"I got this," Josiah said as he flexed his nonexistent muscles.

Casey lowered the boy to the ground and watched as he reached for his grandmother as they made their way through the airport entrance.

"I love you guys," Casey whispered as he choked back tears. He returned to his vehicle when his mother and son were no longer visible.

Bailey

When Bailey arrived at the office on Wednesday morning, she was greeted by a flurry of emails and messages. The Oilers' starting wide receiver requested a trade. As a part of the marketing and communications team, player operations aren't ordinarily a part of Bailey's wheelhouse; however, he was scheduled to participate in a cancer awareness event that the team organized in collaboration with the American Football League. Grabbing a notepad and pen for notes, Bailey read through the email conversation in her inbox. From what Bailey gathered, her boss, Johnathan, was upset that the Player Ops Director would initially approve Marcus Sims to participate in public events when he had been displeased with the team and management for renegotiating his contract.

Bailey checked the PR events calendar to see which prominent players could participate. Different from local events, Bailey could not replace Marcus with just anyone. The national press would be present since the AFL was a partner for this event. She needed someone who commanded attention, was well liked by the general public, and was charismatic. "Ugh," Bailey groaned to herself. Only two other players fit the bill and one of them she wanted to keep her distance from.

A ping from her computer alerted Bailey to a new message from the organization's interoffice messaging system. "Great," Bailey whispered as she rolled her eyes after reading the message. Taking a deep breath to calm her spirit, Bailey replied to the message by confirming her availability in a half-hour. She hoped the meeting would be fruitful and that she would have some good news to share with Johnathan when they met later that afternoon.

Bailey's nerves were on edge, so instead of continuing to work at her desk, she decided to locate a conference room and work there until her meeting. She messaged Casey again to inform him where they would meet and how to find the junior conference room. She reworked the presentation for the cancer awareness event to complement the pending conversation. Though she knew how she wanted to use the time for her business needs, she had no idea why Casey wished to meet with her.

A knock on the door interrupted Bailey's thoughts, and she scanned the room for a clock to confirm the time. "Come in," she called out.

"Hi, Ms. Bailey," Casey chirped as he pushed through the door. "Thank you for meeting with me," he said as he closed the door behind him and walked toward the medium-sized conference table, taking the seat perpendicular to Bailey.

"Hi Mr. Christopher", Bailey started, "To what do I owe the pleasure of this meeting?"

"I'm not gonna lie, I knew a meeting would be the best way I could get your attention." Casey answered.

"Humph," Bailey responded, crossing her arms.

"Look, I just wanted to let you know that I understand why you broke things off with me. I spoke to my mama about you and…"

"You told your mother about me?" Bailey interrupted.

"I did. That's the point. I was furious when I saw you with your boyfriend in the parking lot the other day. I felt betrayed that you would bring another man up here and you know I'm digging you," Casey said.

"Mr. Christopher, I don't think this is an appropriate time or place for this conversation. I apologize for my previous lack of judgement. I should have never entertained the idea of dating you," Bailey offered.

Casey grew frustrated, raising his voice, "Bailey!" he paused before going on, "Can you, for one minute put your professional front aside? I'm trying to have a real conversation with you."

Bailey took a beat to consider her options and use the situation to her advantage, "Okay, but you have to do something for me."

"Sure. What is it?" Casey asked.

"I'll tell you after we finish your discussion. You just need to say yes to what I am going to ask you after that."

With a stone face, Casey was in disbelief that the woman sitting next to him was leveraging work, "Okay, sure," Casey responded flatly.

"Thank you," Bailey said warmly, "please continue."

"Like I said, I was upset to see you in the parking lot with ole boy. As much as I would like to date you, I respect you for protecting your career. I wouldn't be able to forgive myself if your career took a hit because we were dating." Casey leaned forward to rest his forearms on the conference table, "You're dope, and I'm attracted to you; however, as long as we're both with the Oilers, I know we can't be together. I wanted you to know this, so it won't be awkward around here."

Weighing his words, Bailey was pleased that Casey finally got it. "Thank you", she offered.

Casey continued, "…romance aside, you are a dope person, and I would like to be friends." Bailey raised her eyebrow quizzically. "Just regular friends," Casey clarified with a chuckle, "…and with whatever limits you feel comfortable with."

Bailey opened her mouth, then quickly closed it to consider her words a beat longer. "First, thank you for acknowledging where I am coming from. I don't hate you, so you're good with me." Bailey paused, "I think we can try to be friends, especially since I don't have many in the area. And, as my friend, I need you to fill in for the cancer awareness event at the end of the month."

"Wow!" Casey laughed as he ran his hands through his locs. "You don't waste no time I see."

"Not at all," Bailey snickered, "Marcus is no longer available, and we need another star. I know you were heavily engaged with the youth initiatives, but this one is less demanding."

"Is that right?" Casey asked.

"Yes," she said, turning her laptop for Casey to view with her, "this event is in collaboration with the league, and all you'd need to do is take a few pictures and give a short speech," she said while flipping through the slides.

"Bet," Casey said, raising his fist for a dap.

"Thank you," Bailey responded, raising her fist to formalize the agreement.

****

Bailey getting Casey to agree to the cancer awareness event made for a successful meeting with Johnathan that afternoon. It also gave her enough cushion for her to leave work early. Bailey needed to swing by the dry bar to get a quick wash and flat iron, but first wanted to go home and shower. Mike was supposed to pick her up at six-thirty that evening, and now she did not have to rush and compete with the San Diego evening commute traffic. The dry bar was a 10-minute walk from her apartment, so once she showered and changed, she'd stroll over. By her estimation, Bailey anticipated being ready on time.

Assessing her hair and makeup in the bathroom mirror, Bailey was pleased with the look. She asked the stylist to put barrel curls in her hair instead of doing a bone-straight flat-iron. She chose to keep a natural look, using warm corals to brighten her eyes and a nude glossy lip. Bailey slipped into a copper sequined dress with a round neck, spaghetti straps, and a thigh-high split. She was excited for Mike's company gala, if for no reason other than she enjoyed dressing up. This would be the first time since her sorority's annual gala that she could wear a gown.

Mike was speechless when Bailey opened the door. "You look stunning," he complimented.

"Thank you," Bailey responded sweetly. "Let me grab my clutch and we can head out," she continued.

"I feel like I am going to prom all over again with the prettiest girl at the school," Mike chuckled as he escorted Bailey out of her building to his vehicle.

"Hush," Bailey teased, "you probably say that to all the women you take to these things."

"Actually," Mike paused, "this is the first time I'm bringing a date to a work event. I normally hang with some of the guys and crack jokes the entire time".

"Oh!" Bailey responded as she weighed the magnitude of his admission.

"Looks like tonight I will be fighting everyone off of you," he continued.

"It will be fine," Bailey said as she gently kissed Mike's cheek before getting into his truck. After confirming Bailey was secured in the vehicle, he closed the door and strode to the driver's side to begin the night's adventure.

Monica

Monica was glad to be back home in Houston. She truly enjoyed her time in San Diego. The impromptu visit from Kenny was precisely what she needed. Though they had only been dating for a few months, Kenny took every opportunity to let Monica know she was important to him. For the first time, Monica understood what it felt like to be treated like a queen. While Casey could afford whatever Monica's heart desired, he stopped treating her like she was the remarkable woman in his life. With Kenny, she never had to worry about where she stood; he was consistent day in and day out.

With her relationship with Kenny growing stronger each day, Monica knew it was time to talk with Casey about allowing their son Josiah to meet Kenny. She also knew it was time to have the conversation with Casey after their awkward run-in at Bistecca in San Diego. She could see the hurt in his face, which was puzzling to her because he was the one who had ended their relationship. Monica resolved that she would always have love for the man she shared a son with and with whom, until recently, she had spent her entire adult life.

Checking the time on her computer, Monica permitted herself to take a break from studying. It was seven in the evening in California, and she hoped Casey was available for the much-needed co-parenting conversation. She picked up her phone which was resting on the end table beside the couch and scrolled through her contacts. She pressed the phone icon next to Casey's name and put the call on speaker.

"Hey," Monica said when Casey answered the phone.

"What's up," he responded.

"So," Monica stalled as she fished for her earbuds on the couch, "You know that Kenny and I have been seeing each other for a little while and things have become serious for us," taking one of the buds from its cradle, she placed it in her right ear switching the connection from the speaker to Bluetooth. "So before introducing Josiah to Kenny, I wanted to let you know and have a conversation with you to see if you had any concerns about it," Monica concluded.

"What?" Casey responded, confused, "Kenny hasn't met Josiah yet?"

"No," Monica responded. "Why would I introduce Kenny to Josiah without talking to you first?"

"Oh, I don't know," Casey responded. "Y'all looked cozy when I saw y'all in the restaurant last time, so I figured y'all already been playing family."

"Casey, I really wish you knew me better than that," Monica sighed. "Just know I'm not going to have any and everybody around my child. And, I certainly wouldn't have anyone around my child without discussing it with you first. I think it's important as JoJo's parents that we have at least that amount of respect for one another," Monica paused, "…you know, to at least inform the other person when we're going to introduce our child to our new partners," Monica said.

"You're right," Casey agreed. "Honestly, I just didn't think about it. I mean, I'm not dating, and I didn't even know you were dating until I saw you, so you know," Casey paused, "And I know things ended badly, and our communication hasn't been the best."

"It's improving though," Monica reassured.

"I wanted to tell you that I appreciate you for being a good mother to our son and for being a good person to co-parent with. I appreciate you and I know that I haven't told you that before and I apologize for that. So, if you and Kenny are taking your relationship to the next level you certainly have my blessing to introduce him to JoJo."

Monica looked at the phone to see who she was talking to. She couldn't recall the last time Casey apologized to her, sang her praises, or been humble enough to acknowledge his shortcomings. Monica didn't know what was happening with Casey, but she would not interrupt him.

"If there's anything I can do to improve your life and support your relationship, just let me know," Casey offered.

"Thank you, Casey; I appreciate your support, and I appreciate you, too. Josiah is very lucky to have you as a father. Look at us being adults and getting along," Monica joked.

"Ha," Casey laughed, "you're right. You gotta thank my mom for my coming around."

"I adore your mom; she's an amazing woman," Monica shared.

"She loves you too," Casey admitted, "I didn't realize you two were running around like Laverne and Shirley."

"Oh," Monica paused, "she is JoJo's grandmother, and she and I always got along. There was no reason to exclude her from our lives. You just didn't want me," Monica laughed.

Pierced by her words, Casey was overcome by guilt. "Monica?"

"What's up?" she answered.

"I'm sorry. You deserved better from me," Casey apologized.

"Thank you, Casey, for acknowledging that," Monica paused, "I have better now, and though the picture doesn't look like what we imagined when we were kids, we'll always be family."

"So, can we be friends?" Casey asked.

"Yes, silly! I stopped being mad at you a long time ago. I'm good, you're good, we're all good," Monica reassured.

"Thank you," Casey responded soberly.

"Well, it's getting late for me. Let me get off this phone. I'll talk to you later," Monica informed Casey.

"Good night," Casey replied.

"Night."

Monica

Kenny arranged to take Monica and Josiah to a basketball game; the Houston Stars were taking on the Dallas Bluebonnets in their preseason opener. Monica was confident Kenny and JoJo would get along and hoped their initial meeting would set the foundation for the future. She believed attending a basketball game would be the perfect buffer if things did not go as well as expected.

Monica met Kenny in the VIP parking lot at the Stars arena. He had arranged for VIP access and a parking pass after Monica informed him that she preferred meeting at the arena versus him picking her and Josiah up at their house. Entering the parking lot Monica immediately located Kenny's Mercedes. There weren't many cars in the parking lot yet, so she cut across the aisles and parked grill to grill with Kenny. He walked to the driver's side of the car and opened the door for Monica to exit. "Hey," Monica said as she gave Kenny a tight hug, "let me get JoJo from his seat."

"Sure," Kenny responded as he followed her to rear passenger side of the SUV.

Taking a deep breath to compose herself, she opened the door for the moment of truth. Having unbuckled the chest harness of his booster seat Monica released the lower buckle to free Josiah's legs. "Momma, who is that?" Josiah asked while pointing at Kenny.

"This is mommy's friend, Mr. Kenny. He wanted to meet you, so he got us tickets to the game," Monica answered.

"Oh!" Josiah paused, "Hi Mr. Kenny" the boy greeted with a large smile.

Squatting to be leveled with the young boy, "Hi Josiah," Kenny stuck out his hand to formalize the introduction. Josiah looked at the hand curiously before imitating Kenny and sticking out his hand.

"I got us courtside seats if that's okay with you," Kenny informed the young boy as he stood up.

"It's fine," the boy said gleefully.

Josiah reached for Kenny's hand as they made their way to the arena entrance; Monica's heart smiled as she observed her son take to her man. "This could work," she thought to herself as her son chatted up Kenny leaving her two steps behind. Kenny briefly broke his focus from Josiah to flash Monica a reassuring smile.

****

Josiah, Monica, and Kenny went to Pappadeaux for dinner after the game. The Stars lost but that didn't stop the little boy's excitement. "That game was awesome," Josiah shared exuberantly.

"I'm glad you liked it baby," Monica replied.

"This was the best day ever!" Josiah exclaimed as he showed his mother and Kenny the signed basketball he was holding. "All of the players signed it," he went on.

Kenny informed Monica that he had a surprise for Josiah, but he did not go into detail. After the game, she and Josiah were excited when they were escorted to the hall outside of the players' locker room. The team's star player, Jared Knicks, appeared from the locker room and presented Josiah with the game ball with signatures from all the players and coaches.

Kenny really tried to make the day special for Josiah and Monica. Josiah could not get enough of talking about meeting players, taking pictures and his beloved basketball. Memories are important to Monica and this one facilitated by Kenny was quickly climbing the charts.

Monica excused herself after the waiter took their order, "I need to go the restroom. JoJo, do you need to go?"

"No mama," Josiah answered.

Monica turned her gaze to Kenny, "He's fine," Kenny reassured.

"Thank you," Monica replied before turning for the ladies' room.

Kenny watched as Monica walked off; when she was no longer in his line of vision, he turned his attention to the little boy that was sitting next to him in the corner booth.

"So, JoJo" Kenny started, "you know I like your mother, right?"

"I know" Josiah responded quickly. Entirely too quick to understand, Kenny thought to himself.

"One day I want to marry her. Would that be okay with you?" Kenny asked. The young boy was confused about the question but figured he was enjoying himself with his mother's new friend, so he agreed.

"Sure." Josiah answered.

Kenny engaged Josiah in a 5-year old's conversation discussing all his favorite things. Kenny was listening so intently as Josiah was describing the design of his bedroom that he had not noticed Monica had returned.

"What are you two fellas talking about," Monica asked while sliding into the booth next to Josiah?

Stopping mid-sentence Josiah answered, "Mr. Kenny wants to marry you."

"Oh," Monica said as she darted her eyes to Kenny.

Bailey

The cancer awareness event was becoming a thorn in Bailey's side. She managed to get a replacement with little incident, now she was getting word that Marcus Sims wanted back in. Bailey needed to know who the keynote speaker was going to be so she could finalize the event collateral. Jonathan had been in constant communication with the Player Operations Director and had not reached a resolution.

"Hey, Jonathan, you got a minute?" Bailey asked standing in his office's doorway.

"Sure Bailey. What's up?" He countered.

"Have you gotten word about who's going to be the speaker for the cancer event next week? I need to finalize the program and get things going with the printers. It's getting close," she informed him.

"Not yet." Jonathan started, "I have a call with Harvey at two this afternoon."

"Okay. Perhaps, both Marcus and Casey could be the special guests. I know it's not common to have two keynote speakers for these events, but…" Jonathan interrupted Bailey midsentence.

"That actually might work" Jonathan raved. "Can you prepare the layout with both guys and send it to me for review," he asked.

"I already have that done, you should have it in your email in about five minutes," Bailey reassured.

"Where would we be without you," Jonathan gushed. "Let me get Harvey on the phone and I'll get back to you with my feedback."

"Sounds good," Bailey turned on her heels to exit her boss' office.

****

"You are killing it at work" Mike cheered as he raised his beer to salute Bailey on her recent success.

"Thank you," she responded before taking a sip of her wine.

Once Jonathan confirmed that her proposal for the double keynote speaker was approved by the Player Ops Department, Bailey invited Mike to happy hour in the

Gaslamp. Counting that as a major victory in a dicey situation, Bailey wanted to celebrate the occasion. Her regular partner in happy hour crime Sierra, was not available so she reached out to Mike.

"When is the event again?" Mike asked.

"Next week," Bailey answered.

"It's an evening thing, right?"

"Uh, yeah," Bailey hesitated unsure of Mike's line of questioning. "Why do you ask?" she followed up.

"I was just wondering if this was one of those things where you could bring a plus one" Mike inquired.

"Some of my colleagues are bringing a guest, but I don't typically do that for work events" Bailey answered earnestly.

"So, I can't accompany you at work and see what a bad ass you are?" Mike asked outright.

Slowly shaking her head, Bailey replied honestly, "No."

Detecting a shift in Mike's mood, Bailey wondered why he would be offended that she would not invite him to a work function. She started to open her lips to probe further but decided to lift her glass of wine to her mouth for a sip instead.

The remainder of the evening felt forced and uncomfortable for Bailey. She tried to have casual conversation with Mike, however he appeared less than enthusiastic. The light conversation dissipated into phone watching and sporadic comments.

"I'm going to head out," Mike announced.

"Okay," Bailey acknowledged breaking contact with her phone.

"You're not leaving too?" Mike asked.

"Not yet, I am going to stay a while," Bailey stated while rotating in her seat to stand. "I'll call you when I get home," Bailey reassured him as she leaned in for a hug.

Bailey released her embrace when she felt Mike's reluctance to join her in a hug. Stepping back, she smoothed over her clothes. "I'll see you later," she offered before sliding back into her seat.

"Yeah," he snorted before turning to walk away.

Casey

Public speaking was never an issue for Casey, however, he found himself shaking with nerves while seated at the table waiting to be introduced by the mistress of ceremonies. Seated at his table was his teammate and co-keynote honoree Marcus Sims and his wife, Assistant Player Ops Director, Josh, with his date, two cancer survivors with their guest and Bailey.

Casey didn't know if he was nervous because he didn't want to say the wrong thing or if he wanted to impress Bailey. She was beautiful, incredibly smart, and although he had agreed to be platonic friends, a part of him longed for her. Every opportunity he had; Casey basked in Bailey's presence. She wore a black square neck tea length cocktail dress adorned with a single strand of pearl necklace and pearl drop earrings. Bailey wore her hair bone straight with a middle part. Her simple look was stunning, and Casey did all he could to contain himself. He cursed himself for arriving late and thereby not being able to grab a seat next to her. He imagined that she smelled delightful, and he committed to himself that he would get close enough to her before the night was over to find out.

Casey was shocked when he received a standing ovation from the audience at the end of his speech. When he arrived back at his table a coy smile crept up his face as Bailey mouthed "great job" to him. While he was partial to the kid-friendly events that focused on being active Casey realized that he had underestimated how enjoyable the formal events could be; though, he did not like wearing suits or dress shoes.

****

After the cancer awareness event ended, Casey made the decision to linger in the foyer in hopes of catching Bailey. She remained inside the event hall once the event concluded, and the guests filed out to the parking lot. Casey positioned himself along the far wall that was to the left of the banquet hall entryway where those exiting into the foyer wouldn't see him right away. He'd hope the advantage would allow him to spot Bailey first while being discreet to anyone else needing to exit the building.

"Hey, Ms. Bailey," Casey called out when he spotted her leaving the event hall unaccompanied.

"H…Hey," she responded startled by Casey's presence.

"Where is your boyfriend?" he asked.

"He's not my boyfriend," Bailey replied looking around the foyer.

"Oh, could have fooled me," Casey prodded.

"Well, you're wrong. Thank you very much," Bailey sneered.

"How do you think it went?" Bailey asked, changing the subject.

"Man, I'm not even really trying to talk about all that right now" Casey admitted.

"Okay, sounds good," Bailey started, "I'll have an evaluation for both of you guys tomorrow anyway, I was just trying to get some feedback right away." Bailey went on as she leaned towards the building entrance, "On any account thank you again. I am going to head out now."

"Do you mind giving me a ride?" Casey asked.

"A ride?" Bailey asked puzzled. "Why do you need a ride?"

"I took a car here instead of driving myself and I was going to take it back but since you're right here I figured you can give an old friend a ride home," Casey admitted.

"I'm not sure about that," Bailey hesitated. She was mindful to remain vigilant about the optics of being too close with any of the players on the team. Considering Casey was still one of her biggest crushes and that they had even gone out on a date, the last thing she wanted was to be seen driving around with him. "I mean; I'll wait with you while your car comes back but I don't really feel comfortable driving with you."

"I hear you; but I'm not just anybody, we're friends, remember? Plus, how do you think my coach is going to feel if I arrive late tomorrow because I am so tired from this event because my car came late," Casey coerced.

"Are you blackmailing me?" Bailey asked.

"Blackmail, white male, call it whatever you want."

"Unbelievable," Bailey said as she rolled her eyes in disbelief. "This is ridiculous," she continued.

"Well, the longer we stand here the more eyes are going to see that you and I are talking" Casey rationalized.

"I really don't know what to do with you. Is this how you get your way? Bailey asked.

"Get my way?" Casey feigned hurt. "Most people just do what I say. There's never any jockeying or negotiating," Casey boasted.

"See, now you're starting to talk like an arrogant athlete that's full of himself. You sir, who need a ride home should humble yourself. Or better yet, you can catch a cab, Uber, or a Lyft, I don't care".

"Really? That's how you gonna do me?" Casey asked.

"Nope! That's how you're doing yourself" Bailey said as she exited the building.

Casey was in awe that Bailey would leave him standing there after he asked for a ride home. Pulling his phone out of his pants pocket Casey began to contact the car company to dispatch a driver as he walked slowly to the entrance of the foyer. He decided to wait for his car inside the glass double doors because it was a chilly night, and he didn't have an overcoat.

Playing on his phone Casey looked up abruptly when he heard a car horn; and a small smile crept along his face. Pressing his way through the double doors Casey made his way to the waiting vehicle and got in.

"I thought you left me" Casey quizzed the driver as he adjusted the passenger seat for additional leg room and to engage the seat belt.

"I did leave you," the driver said.

"Well, you came back," Casey said as he pointed his finger at the side of the driver's face.

"That, I did. So where do you live?" Bailey asked.

"Chula Vista," Casey informed her. "Do you know how to get over there?" he asked.

"Yes," she replied.

"Perfect," Casey started, "Just make your way toward Chula Vista and then I will give you the turn-by-turn directions".

"Whatever" Bailey grumbled.

"So, this is what it feels like to be in a drug dealer's car?" Casey kidded.

"Wow! Really?" Bailey exclaimed. "I'm giving you a ride in my nice vehicle and you're going to accuse me of being a drug dealer?"

"Well, not you but your boyfriend," Casey clarified. "Because, like I said before and now sitting in this car and seeing how tricked out it is, this is definitely a drug dealer's car."

"Like I told you before, my dad got me this car for my graduation," Bailey countered.

"Mystery solved! Your dad is a drug dealer," Casey teased.

"Get out," Bailey said as she slowed the vehicle down at a stop sign.

"You would put me out on the side of the road?" Casey complained.

"If you keep it up, absolutely," she threatened.

"Well, let me be quiet then and let's turn the music up," Casey said as he went to adjust the controls of Bailey's audio system.

Immediately popping his hand Bailey yelled, "Boy, what is wrong with you? I give you a ride, you judge my car, and now you're touching my radio. You know the rules; don't ever touch a person's radio," Bailey admonished.

"So, what am I supposed to do?" Casey asked, "You just want me to sit here in the passenger seat quiet, not listening to nothing and can't talk to you?"

"Absolutely."

"I'm hungry," Casey complained.

"Hungry?" Bailey asked.

"Can you take me to In-N-Out?" Casey asked.

"Sir! Do I look like a Lyft to you?" Bailey questioned.

"Not at all. Because if you were a Lyft, you would be getting zero stars from me," Casey teased.

"You know what!" Bailey exclaimed.

Casey could see that he was getting under Bailey's skin. He'd hope she found his antics appealing.

"Where is the In-N-Out," Bailey asked.

"There is one, an exit before my house that you can take me to," Casey responded.

Taking a deep sigh Bailey snorted "I see you don't care if I'm late to work tomorrow because every in and out has a line around the corner always and I still need to get home which is on the other side of town."

"You could always stay with..." Casey started.

"Nope," Bailey said raising her finger to Casey's face cutting him off before he could finish his sentence.

Casey took advantage of the long drive-thru line to show his true personality and learn more about Bailey by initiating a game of twenty-one questions. Bailey was not enthusiastic about the game initially, but after a few rounds she warmed up to it.

Casey did not want to get out of the car when she pulled up to his home, but he knew she had a 25-minute drive home, and it was approaching midnight. "Let me know when you get home," Casey requested as he got out of Bailey's car. He stood in his driveway and watched as Bailey drove off. He didn't turn for his house until the rear lights of her vehicle were no longer visible.

Bailey

Music from Bailey's enhanced sound system boomed from her car as she made the turn into the Oilers parking lot. Under normal circumstances Bailey would lower her music, but today was her birthday and she was feeling fabulous. The music's bass reverberated through her body creating an energy that could sustain her for weeks.

Her morning had been filled with surprises; she received a surprise special delivery from Mike and her father. Bailey loved receiving gifts, and she was the happiest when it came to surprises. Mike ordered a floral arrangement and Build-A-Bear while her father sent her favorite edible arrangement and balloons.

"Aren't you a special one," Bailey's boss commented while taking in the display at her desk.

"These are from my dad," Bailey shared pointing to the balloons "and these are from a guy I'm seeing," she continued.

"Looks like I should have ordered a fancier lunch" Jonathan teased.

"You know I'm not even like that. I appreciate you for even thinking about me on my birthday," Bailey reassured.

Looking at his watch Jonathan offered a final reminder before leaving Bailey's desk, "Don't forget to meet me in the break room at noon."
"Sounds good," Bailey confirmed.

Bailey busied herself for an hour, less with work and more with fielding text messages and social media messages wishing her a happy birthday. She always liked to thank people individually who took the time to acknowledge her. She anticipated being less available during her party and prepping for it, so she wanted to get to as many people as possible before the day grew late.

$$*********************$$

"Happy Birthday," a crowd sang to Bailey as she walked into the break room.
"Oh, my goodness! This is so beautiful" Bailey said as she wiped an unexpected tear before it fell from her eye.

"Thank you all so very much. I cannot believe this. Jonathan, I am going to get you."

Jonathan had arranged for their department to have a mini surprise birthday celebration for Bailey. Jonathan told Bailey that he would be ordering lunch for the two of them and when noon arrived, she should meet him in the break room. When she walked in, she saw that it wasn't just Jonathan in there, but her entire department was in attendance and just about everyone on the floor was crowded into the spacious break area. She spotted a sheet cake, cupcakes and cookies along with boxes of pizza, wings, salad and breadsticks. Bailey recalled telling Jonathan pizza was one of her favorite foods, but she hadn't expected him to remember let alone throw her a party.

Jonathan's expression of gratitude warmed Bailey's heart. "You are very special to us around here," Jonathan shared while standing on the front row of the crowd. "We wanted to make your birthday special," he concluded.

"Thank you, Jonathan, you have truly been the best boss ever," Bailey thanked him.

"Plus," Geneva said pressing her way to the front of the room, she placed a "birthday girl" sash and a tiara on

Bailey's head. "Jonathan did have some help, you know," she concluded.

"Of course, he did," Bailey replied hugging her work friend.

"Well, happy birthday Bailey" one of the guys in the back yelled out, "it's time to eat!"

"Absolutely! Thank you all so much! Please, eat and enjoy."

"Whoa, whoa, whoa, whoa, whoa," Geneva interrupted, "before you all start stuffing your faces it's only right that we sing the birthday song". Ushering Bailey to the center table in front of the cake, Geneva began singing "happy birthday to you…" as everyone in the break room started to join in the chorus.

Bailey remained in the break room chatting with her co-workers and sharing her plans for an hour with Geneva right by her side. "Well, this has been real. It's time that I get back to my post," Geneva announced.

"Sounds good. I should do the same." Bailey agreed. "I'm going to take a piece of cake down to Sally."

"Oh, I can do that for you", a colleague offered.

"It's fine. I haven't seen her all week so I'm going to grab a few slices of pizza for her and some cake and take it down to her" Bailey countered.

"All right girl, I'll see you when you come back up."

Unsure of what type of pizza Sally would want of the remaining available options, cheese, veggie, pepperoni and sausage and Hawaiian, Bailey loaded a slice of each on a paper plate. She then filled a second plate with cake, covering them both with paper plates. She then proceeded to the elevator bank and pressed the button for the main floor.

Sally's face beamed when she saw Bailey exit the elevator. "Well don't you have your hands full" Sally commented.

"Indeed, I do, and I am so glad you are here, I've been missing you all week", Bailey responded.

"I know, missy. You've been arriving early and leaving late again?" Sally asked.

"I have," Bailey admitted. "Anyway, this is for you" Bailey shared as she set both plates on Sally's elevated desk.

"For me?" Sally questioned, "What's the occasion?"

"It's my birthday and Jonathan planned a surprise party for me upstairs. Since you are one of my favorite people here, I just had to make sure that you got some pizza and some cake." Bailey admitted.

"Thank you, sweetheart. That is so kind of you and happy birthday. How old are we turning this year, 16?" Sally replied.

Laughing, Bailey shook her head "Now you know I'm not turning 16, I'm turning 21". The two women laughed in unison. "I didn't know what kind of pizza you like, so I brought you a slice of each and here's a piece of cake. It should be enough for you and your husband," Bailey shared.

Sally removed the top plate that was covering the plate holding the cake and said "Oh my! This is way more than enough cake for me and Bill. He'll eat most of this you know. I'm watching my womanly figure" Sally giggled.

"Well, I have to get going if I plan on leaving early today; and I can only do that if I finish up what I need to do upstairs. But I wanted to make sure you had these," Bailey shared.

"Thanks again," Sally offered, "I'll have something for you before you leave today, so on your way out be sure to stop by my desk".

"Absolutely," Bailey agreed.

****

As promised Jonathan allowed Bailey to leave work 2 hours early so she could go home and prepare for her party that evening. Bailey's arms were filled with the gifts that were delivered as well as the gifts she received from Jonathan and Geneva as she walked through the lobby of Oilers Central. "Wow! You have a lot there," Sally observed as Bailey walked toward her desk. "I was wondering who all of these things were for. I should have known when you came down earlier."

"I know right," Bailey agreed, "These are from my dad, he always sends me something for my birthday. These are from a guy I'm dating," Bailey shared as she pointed to the edible arrangement, balloons and flowers.

"That's some guy you got there Ms. Bailey; you might want to hold on to him" Bailey chuckled at Sally's comment.

"We'll see about that. I don't know about him just yet" she replied honestly.

"Here you go, this is from me and Bill," Sally said as she handed Bailey a card.

Bailey received the card and cradled it between her thumb and the flower vase, "Thank you so much Sally. You see, my hands are full but as soon as I get home, I'm going to open it."

"Of course, dear, no rush," Sally reassured.

"I really appreciate you thinking about me" Bailey said as she began walking towards the exit. She continued to struggle with her birthday haul due to the wind blowing the balloons out of control.

"Let me help you," a familiar voice called out.

Peeking around the flowers, Bailey saw Casey getting out of his truck. "How is it that you always seem to be in the parking lot when I'm in the parking lot," Bailey asked.

"Maybe because we work at the same place," Casey guffawed.

Bailey rolled her eyes "If you say so. I just find it real strange that we always seem to meet in the parking lot."

"Not true," Casey disagreed "we've met in the hall a few times."

"I guess," Bailey responded, "As luck would have it, today I'm not even going to fight with you. I can absolutely use a second pair of hands."

"What do you have here anyway?" Casey asked.

"These are some gifts that came for me today for my birthday," Bailey responded.

"Nice," Casey started, "from your little boyfriend I presume."

"Actually, this is from my dad," Bailey told a partial truth.

"Really? Your dad sent you all of this," Casey mocked.

"I mean some of the stuff is from Mike" Bailey admitted.

"Oh, so I was right," Casey said, "How you just gone try to lie like that."

"Not lying," Bailey replied, "it's just not your business."

"If I'm helping you…," Casey started.

"No, no, no, no honey," Bailey interrupted, "you offered so let's be very clear about that."

"Anyway," Casey started while placing the large floral arrangement on the trunk of Bailey's car.

"Anyway, what Casey? I know you got something smart to say" Bailey chastised.

"No, I'm going to let you have it. You're the birthday girl, so I'm going to let you have it." Casey backed down.

"Why thank you Mr. Christopher, it is much appreciated," Bailey feigned a southern belle accent.

"So, what do you got planned tonight? Is there going to be a birthday dinner or something?" Casey asked.

"Of course! We are going down to The Hot Spot in the Gaslamp. I'm having a little party there" Bailey answered.

"You didn't invite me?" Casey asked feigning hurt and placing his hand over his heart.

"Now you absolutely know why I did not invite you" Bailey replied. "But…" Bailey started "If you want to stop by it is a public place, you most certainly can," Bailey shared.

"You mean I can come to your birthday party with a secondhand invitation? I would love to," Casey pouted, "but I can't because I have plans tonight."

"So much drama with you Casey, so much drama," Bailey said as she shook her head in disbelief.

"I appreciate your help getting to my car, but I must get going. A lady has a nail and hair appointment, and I can't be late."

"Okay Ms. Bailey. It was lovely seeing you. Happy birthday and enjoy the rest of your day." Casey walked away as Bailey was still placing her gifts in the backseat of her car. When she stood up after fighting with the balloons Bailey found Casey was out of sight. That wasn't so bad, she thought to herself.

Casey

Pacing across his living room, Casey fought with himself on whether he should attend Bailey's birthday party at The Hot Spot. She did invite me, Casey thought to himself. How would it look if I just showed up, he went on. Casey meandered to the kitchen island where a luxury shopping bag sat. He rubbed his fingers across the ornate bag before walking away in a huff. "Fuck it," Casey mumbled to himself. Pulling his phone from his sweatpants pocket he began pressing buttons, Casey crossed the living room and climbed the stairs.

"Hey man, what you got going on tonight," Casey asked the person on the other end of the line.

"Say, do you want to hit the Gaslamp with me tonight?" Casey walked into his closet looking for a casual yet eye catching ensemble.

"Sounds good. I'll be there in an hour," Casey confirmed before clicking the call off.

****

"Man, this is crazy," Jamal said from the passenger seat of Casey's blacked out S-Class Mercedes Benz. "Does she even know you are coming to her party?" Jamal followed up.

"I told her I was busy," Casey admitted. "But she did invite me," he quickly countered.

"Man, I hope you're not getting me into some mess," Jamal asked cautiously.

"Naw. Plus, as big as we are we'll be fine," Casey reassured.

"Yeah," Jamal retorted, "Until someone figures out who we are, and they want to slap us with a lawsuit. You, my friend, will be paying my legal fees."

"Be positive, man. We're going to the birthday party of a colleague, we *both* work with her," Casey assured.

"Didn't you say that she had a boyfriend," Jamal asked for clarity.

"Trust me, we will only be there for a bit. We'll go, have a drink, I'll give her her gift and then we can be out," Casey shared.

"Alright bro, I'm holding you to it," Jamal replied, "my girl was not pleased with me going out with you tonight."

"I'll send flowers tomorrow," Casey chuckled.

Casey found a parking space down the block from The Hot Spot. He grabbed the gift bag from the back seat and began to walk in stride with Jamal up the block.

DJ Franz had the crowd jumping. He was playing all of the latest club hits when Casey and Jamal entered The Hot Spot. Casey made his way to the bar and ordered a couple of beers for Jamal and himself. When the bartender returned with two long necks, Casey pulled a twenty dollar bill out of his wallet and placed it in the bartender's hand. "No change," he yelled over the music.

Casey turned from the bar and rested his back against it. He focused his eyes and began scanning the room searching for Bailey, "Aye man," Casey said hitting Jamal on the arm, "they're they go," he said pointing up to the mezzanine.

"You ready bro," Jamal asked.

Casey crossed the dance floor and ascended the stairs to the mezzanine to join Bailey's party. Pausing at the top of the landing Casey surveyed the crowd; he identified a face from the Oilers administrative office, Bailey's boyfriend Mike, and moving gracefully in the middle of the crowd in a dazzling red dress, Bailey. Casey stood enamored as she expertly moved her body to the music. He imagined that he was dancing with her and that they were moving their bodies in sync.

"Hello," Jamal stated, "anyone home?" he asked while waving his hand in front of Casey's face.

"Oh, yeah," Casey hesitated. "Let's go," he commanded as he began walking toward Bailey's group.

Squeezing through the small crowd, Casey reached for Bailey's elbow to get her attention. "Hey. Hey! You're here?" Bailey asked astonished. "I didn't think you would come," she continued.

Casey could not determine if Bailey was pleased to see him or if she was being polite. He silently cursed himself; he should not have come. Bailey reached in to initiate a hug, "Thank you for coming," releasing her embrace from Casey, Bailey walked over to Jamal and repeated her greeting.

"I see you guys have beer and I know you have a game this weekend, but if you want there is plenty to drink over there," Bailey said as she pointed to the table. Casey eyes followed Bailey's hand when she pointed to their table and a beat later was met with an unwelcoming glare from Mike. To soften the tension Casey raised his beer to salute Mike.

"Here, let me introduce you guys," Bailey offered. To Casey's surprise Bailey's friends and sorority sisters were a fun bunch. No one lingered or attempted to throw themselves on him or Jamal. In most settings women jump at the opportunity to be around professional athletes. Bailey then re-reintroduced Casey to Mike and introduced them to the other guys in attendance who were there because of their wife or girlfriend.

Casey and Jamal chatted with the guys at the table making nice, though Casey could feel Mike was seething below the surface. He did not want to ruin Bailey's night by causing a scene, so he let Mike writhe in anger. About forty-five minutes after crashing Bailey's birthday party, Casey excused himself citing that he needed to rest in preparation for their upcoming game.

With all the energy the night brought, Casey almost forgot to give Bailey her gift. "We about to head out," he bent down to whisper in her ear. "This is for you," he said handing Bailey the posh gift bag, "open it when you get home," he instructed.

"What is it," Bailey asked gleefully looking down into the bag.

"You'll love it, I hope," Casey reassured.

"Well, thank you" Bailey exclaimed, "I'll let you know when I open it."

"Sounds good," Casey replied, "Enjoy the rest of your party."

Exiting the mezzanine level, Casey located the server to order another round of bottles and to pay the full tab. He even left an additional thousand dollars on the tab to cover additional costs and the tip. Casey knew he didn't need to pay for Bailey's party, because she had her own money, and her friends were the professional type, so they were all probably ballers. His ego told him he needed to leave his mark on the evening, so he flexed.

Bailey

After her birthday party at The Hot Spot Mike drove Bailey home and stayed the night. During the drive she sensed agitation from Mike but was far too inebriated to initiate a conversation. Picking her phone up from the bedside table and clicking through it alerted Mike of her consciousness; he vowed to get answers to his questions before leaving Bailey's house.

"Do you want to tell me what last night was all about," Mike demanded.

Bailey sat up slowly in her bed with a pounding headache. "Not particularly. And, why do you have an attitude so early in the morning," Bailey countered.

"Really? You think having that guy show up at your birthday party is not a big deal?" Mike asked.

Biting back her frustration with Mike's insecurities Bailey responded calmly, "Like I have said previously, Casey is a coworker and friend. I ran into him on my way out of work yesterday and mentioned to him where I was having a party when he asked about my birthday plans."

"You must take me for a fool," Mike lashed out, "you say it's nothing going on with you two and yet he's always around. He popped up in the parking lot that day I came to your job. You just so happen to have a late-night work event with him for which I was not invited to, and now he mysteriously shows up to your birthday party; with an expensive gift at that."

"Mike, this is my job, and you know that I work with professional athletes and yes some of them I am friends with. Some more than others, but it means nothing," Bailey shouted back. "These guys live in a world where they are the star, and it is my job to keep them engaged with the real world which means I need to keep them as my ally."

"Honestly, Bailey, you can say what you want but I have eyes," Mike started, "I wish I could believe you, however every time I turn around this guy shows up. So, either you're blind to what is really going on, and I know you're smarter than that, or you must think I am a fool."

Mike looked around the room for his clothes. He spotted them on the chair in the corner of Bailey's room. She must have picked them up and folded them in the early morning hours while he was sleeping, he thought to himself. "You need to think about what it is you really want," Mike said as he stepped into his pants. "You need to come clean about the thing you and Casey have going, or I don't know."

"Come clean? What are you talking about?" Bailey asked while throwing back the covers to get out of the bed, and why are you starting a fight with me on my birthday weekend?"

"You've got to be kidding me," Mike replied while slipping into his shirt. "You're worried about your birthday, and I am telling you how I feel about your friendship with your 'coworker'".

"Mike," Bailey started massaging her temples, "there is nothing to come clean about. You need to let go of whatever story you created in your mind. I cannot be responsible for your insecurities about my career."

Mike was in disbelief of what Bailey had accused him of, "So now I'm insecure? Really, Bailey?"

"What else am I left to believe? You knew where I worked from the jump and now, because a player came to my party last night you are behaving like a jerk, completely ruining the vibes from last night and for the weekend." Bailey sat back down on the bed exhausted with the conversation and feeling defeated. "Do you not have female co-workers?" she asked, "Or is your industry male-dominated?"

"That is not the point, and you know that, Bailey!" Mike criticized. "Yes, I have female friends and colleagues and guess what, I don't buy them jewelry for their birthday."

Bailey was livid, she could not believe Mike would start a fight with her the morning after her birthday because Casey showed up with Jamal Scott and gifted her a diamond necklace. The gift was far too expensive for her to accept, and she planned on returning it at a later time.

"So let me ask you this," Mike followed up, "why did you accept the gift then?"

"And, like I said, I can't control what someone else does." She rebutted.

She planned to return the diamond necklace Casey bought for her, though she had no intention of telling Mike. If he did not trust her then what was it all worth. If she did not work for the Oilers, Bailey would be working for some other professional sports team. If Mike couldn't handle how Bailey interacted with the players, then the two of them would never work.

Mike finished dressing and made his way out of her room. "So, you're just going to leave a conversation you started," Bailey asked.

"There's not much more left to say. I'll hit you up later," Mike offered.

Bailey said nothing else and made no efforts to stop him. She could not believe he had the audacity to have an issue with her job and then walked out despite the conversation not being over. One thing Bailey learned from her father was to never let people see her sweat. Mike would either need to get over his insecurities or leave her alone. Either way, Bailey was committed to her career, and she was not going to jeopardize it for anyone. She picked her phone back up and made a call to her favorite guy.

****

Talking to her dad always made Bailey feel better. He possessed so much wisdom and she was committed to absorbing as much of it as she could. Bailey's father went into protect mode after her mother died. Though he treated her like a princess he made sure she knew how to take care of herself; and if anything serious were to happen she had reinforcement from her brothers and him. Whatever hole Mr. Jones could not fill, he nurtured relationships between Bailey and her aunts, both his and his late wife's sisters.

"Hi dad," Bailey sang soon as her father answered her call.

"Hey baby girl. How are you? Mr. Jones replied.

"I'm good, just recovering from last night."

"Oh really, what did you all do?" Mr. Jones inquired.

"I had a party at The Hot Spot, it's down in the Gaslamp district. On Sundays they have a cigar bar you would love it," Bailey shared.

"I'm pleased to hear you enjoyed celebrating your birthday and that you made it back home safely," Mr. Jones returned.

"Daddy, can I talk to you about something," Bailey sighed.

"Sure, what's on your mind," Mr. Jones comforted.

"You remember that guy I told you I was seeing" Bailey quizzed.

"Sure," Mr. Jones agreed.

"We had an argument this morning about my job. I think he's insecure about where I work," she announced.

"Why would you say that? Things were going great when you spoke of him last," Mr. Jones confirmed.

"Can you believe this morning Mike started a fight with me because one of the players came out to my party and gave me a gift. He has in his mind that something is going on between myself and Casey. I can't keep reassuring him and his ego that there's absolutely nothing going on between Casey and me. I work with professional athletes, and some are my friends. I can't constantly be worried about how Mike feels with each person I encounter," Bailey shared.

"Baby girl you know I love you and you know I always got your back, but you need to be honest with yourself about the situation" Mr. Jones challenged.

"I am being honest," Bailey started.

"Are you really? You and I both know that you have had a crush on Casey Christopher and we both know that you crossed the line and went on a date with him a few months ago. So don't sit here and try to act innocent as if there's nothing going on with you two" Mr. Jones challenged.

"Yeah, but dad I also told you that I ended that situation with him. He respected the fact that my career is very important to me and that I would never blur the lines with him again" Bailey protested.

"Can you honestly say Casey feels nothing for you," Mr. Jones started, "Tell me this, what did Casey buy you for your birthday gift."

Bailey chewed on her bottom lip as she pondered her father's question. Did she feel absolutely nothing for Casey? Or did she just block it out in hopes that her feelings would go away? "Well, he bought me a diamond necklace… but I am going to return it," Bailey replied.

"I have spoiled you," Mr. Jones started, "The fact that Casey is comfortable enough with gifting your expensive jewelry says a lot more than you think." He continued, "And, I will not allow you to be dishonest with me or yourself about the situation with Casey."

"But dad," Bailey started to interrupt.

"But dad, nothing" Mr. Jones cut her off, "Not once have you thought about this from Mike's perspective because you think men should succumb to your every whim. I obviously blame myself and your brothers for this attitude, but you really need to check it."

Bailey was taken aback by her father's tone. She had called him seeking comfort from Mike's overreaction to Casey attending her party and here he was doing the exact opposite. Accountability was something her dad preached to her and her brothers growing up; and while she was not excited to hear what he had to say, Bailey listened closely.

"Bailey, darling, you need to take some time to really think about what's going on in your love life and how to get it under control. One thing you don't want is for your career to ruin your relationships and you end up old and alone. You say that you want to be married and have a family one day; do you want your career to interfere with that" Mr. Jones cautioned.

Sighing, "I don't know if I can go on with Mike and there's no way that I could ever be with Casey" Bailey admitted. "Daddy, can you come down here next week? I miss you and I just want a sense of normalcy," she asked.

"I'll look up airfare and will get back with you before the weekend is up" Mr. Jones confirmed.

"Thanks Daddy. I'll talk to you later. Love you, bye" Bailey said before disconnecting her call.

Bailey

Much to her appreciation, work was calm. The Oilers were in the middle of their season, so news swirled about mid-season player movement. The Oilers had a narrow lead in the division with a 4-3 record. Should they go on to make a playoff run Bailey knew the holidays would be an extremely busy time for her and the organization.

The week leading up to her father's arrival was uneventful. She had not heard from Mike all week despite making two attempts to contact him. She loathed being ignored and felt Mike's inability to communicate or acknowledge her attempts at contact was outrageous. If settling things with Mike wasn't enough, Bailey still needed to return the necklace Casey gifted her with on her birthday. The diamond tennis necklace was exquisite. It was set in rose gold and the diamonds danced under the lights. Bailey found herself admiring the magnificent piece of jewelry every night. She had no idea how many carats the necklace was, but an online search result for a similar style of necklace showed it cost more than twenty grand.

Bailey wanted to spend the weekend alone with her father, however after finding out Mr. Jones would be visiting southern California, Bryce, Bailey's older brother, invited himself along. Mr. Jones withheld this information from Bailey until Friday morning, he knew she would be upset about the change of plans, however he figured she could use the additional love from family at this current time. Her patience was low, and she hoped Bryce would be on his best behavior. He was such a wild card, liable to say or do anything at a moment's notice. She loved Bryce, he had an uncanny way of disarming folks and making them feel relaxed and comfortable. But he was a lot to manage, and Bailey was not in the mood.

****

Bryce and Mr. Jones arrived on the last inbound flight into San Diego airport. Bailey waited curbside at the arrivals gate for her father and brother to emerge with their bags. She was happy the airport police didn't give her a difficult time as she waited. During high traffic hours the airport police prohibit cars from waiting at the arrivals exit doors. With few cars waiting in the area, the authorities did not cause a fuss. When she spotted her father and brother Bailey exited her car to greet them.

"How was your flight," Bailey asked.

"Wretched," Bryce answered hastily while passing Bailey his carry-on luggage.

"Not short enough," Mr. Jones added while intercepting the luggage hand-off between Bailey and Bryce.

"Bryce complained the whole time?" Bailey asked, responding to her father's assessment of the flight from Oakland to San Diego.

"This guy is a character. I felt bad for the flight crew with his ongoing complaints, like it wasn't a Southwest flight," Mr. Jones shared as he laughed.

"I don't know why you are surprised," Bailey started, "you know Bryce always expects 5-star service," she joined him in laughter while opening the trunk of her car.

"Are you two really talking about me like I am not standing right here," Bryce demanded.

"It wouldn't be right if we talked about you behind your back. Now would it," Mr. Jones countered.

"I'm getting in the car," Bryce squawked, "…and Bailey, I need food," he announced before closing the rear passenger door.

"Your child is a mess," Bailey complained to Mr. Jones, rounding the car for the driver's seat.

"I know," Bailey's father sighed.

Bailey took her father and brother to the Gaslamp for a late-night meal. She considered going to a drive-thru but opted for the lively neighborhood on a Friday night. The men were only in town for two days and she wanted to make the most of their time together. They settled in a pub where they dined on burgers and fries.

Casey

Casey was surprised to receive a call from Bailey over the weekend. He knew whatever she needed to talk about was not work related, if it had been, then she would have contacted him during the week. He had not seen or spoken to Bailey since the night of her party and if he was honest with himself, he had intentionally avoided her. Perhaps she was calling to finally thank him for the necklace he thought to himself. Casey drove himself crazy with speculation as he watched the phone ring in his hand.

"I'll call her back," he said to himself.

What was going on with him, why was he behaving like a pre-pubescent child who had a crush on their schoolteacher. Casey chastised himself for having rising feelings for Bailey. He had promised her and his mother that he would respect her boundaries and maintain a platonic friendship with her.

"Fuck," he yelled out at no one.

His phone dinged indicating that he had an incoming text message. He double tapped the phone screen to wake it up; the notification bar confirmed the message was from

Bailey. Casey desperately wanted to talk to someone about his feelings; his mother would not be pleased, so he knew not to call her. He could call Jamal, but he didn't want to bring him further into the mess that he created. He entered the passcode and clicked on the message to read it in its entirety.

Casey paced his bedroom floor thinking of a response to Bailey's message. She never ceased to amaze him. He wasn't shocked that she wanted to return the gift. He knew that it was too expensive when he purchased it. A part of him wanted to take care of her and give her nice things. He hoped that by doing so, just maybe she would be willing to let down her guard and give him a chance.

In an ongoing text exchange Casey labored to reassure Bailey that the necklace was a modest gift for which he did not spend a lot of money on. It was a lie; he didn't want her to return the gift because of the price tag. Yet, knowing that she researched the necklace drew him in even more. Bailey was thorough, she was principled. He wondered to himself how many women would have taken the jewelry and gone on with their lives. Not Bailey, she was truly special and wanted nothing from him. Well, except for him to leave her alone, which was something he was having a hard time doing.

Bailey

Bailey woke up on Saturday morning to the aroma of breakfast. She either needed to frequent home more or move her dad to San Diego. Mr. Jones was an amazing cook, and Bailey loved it when he cooked for her. Bryce repositioned himself to take up additional bed space when he felt Bailey sit up in the bed, swinging her legs off the side of her bed Bailey grabbed her robe and made her way to the living room.

"That smells wonderful," Bailey shared as she took inventory of the spread.

"Grab a plate," Mr. Jones instructed, "there's sausage, eggs, biscuits and hash browns.".

"You are the best, daddy." Bailey lauded.

Bailey grabbed a plate for herself and her father from the cabinet and forks from the drawer; she then proceeded to fix her plate.

"Go wake your brother," Mr. Jones instructed.

"Ugh! Do I have too," she whined.

"Do you really want to hear his mouth when he wakes up and the food is cold," he countered.

"Good point," Bailey agreed as she exited the kitchen for her bedroom.

Bailey returned to the kitchen with Bryce on her heels.

"You made my plate?" Bryce sang out as he grabbed the plate of food from Bailey's hands that she had just picked up from the kitchen counter.

Bailey made eye contact with her father and began shaking her head. Mr. Jones returned a compassion-filled smile. Bryce was fatiguing at best and an all-out nuisance when fully charged. The family learned long ago to work around him. Bryce was an enigma, he loved fiercely and was available at a moment's notice for anyone he loved, but with that came his demanding boisterous personality.

Mr. Jones and Bailey fixed their plates and joined Bryce at the kitchen table who had begun picking at his food. A traditional man, Mr. Jones scowled at Bryce who immediately placed his fork on the plate and dropped his head so that his father could bless the meal. Once the meal was properly blessed the trio dug into their breakfast.

Bryce interrupted the silence of their mealtime to confirm plans for the day. "So, what are we doing today?" he asked.

"I need to return the necklace Casey gave me for my birthday, but other than that nothing much. It's up to you guys," Bailey offered.

"I'm here to relax and visit my daughter," Mr. Jones chimed in.

"I seen that necklace Bailey" Bryce announced with a side eye.

"You went through my stuff?" Bailey asked annoyed by her brother's lack of respect for boundaries.

"You were talking about its last night, and I just had to see what the big fuss was about," he started.

"And…" Bailey quizzed.

"Girl, you are crazy! If you don't keep that necklace and sell it. How many carats is that thing, 20?" Bryce went on.

"Now, I want to see this infamous necklace too," Mr. Jones turned to Bailey.

"I'll get it!" An excited Bryce got up from the table heading for Bailey's room. He returned a few seconds later with the luxe gift bag, placing it on the table in front of his father.

Bailey was doing her best to contain her frustration. She planned on not showing the necklace to anyone and now her brother had gone through her things showcasing the gaudy neck piece. Mr. Jones wiped his hands on a napkin before lifting the black velvet jewelry box from its bag. Bailey lifted her head from her plate when she heard her father gasp.

"Bailey Anjanae Jones! Child, you should have returned this immediately," Mr. Jones chastised.

"Return?" Bryce was aghast. "She needs to keep that puppy and sell it!"

"Bryce, I know you're being dramatic, so I am going to ignore you," Mr. Jones replied.

"I told you Mike and I had a fight last week. I wasn't up to doing much during the week, which is why I am doing it now," Bailey pleaded.

"Daddy, don't be so rude." Bryce said, "It's impolite to return a gift."

"Bryce…" Mr. Jones interrupted.

"We all know Bailey loves gifts," Bryce teased.

"I already texted him earlier and told him that I would be bringing the necklace to him," Bailey offered. "You guys can ride with me over there and then we can do whatever y'all want."

"You know where he lives?" Bryce exclaimed. "Sis, I don't know who you trying to fool, but you're not fooling me!"

"Bryce," Mr. Jones interjected, "ease up on your sister, why don't you."

Rolling his eyes, Bryce replied, "If you say so."

"Thank you, daddy," Bailey mouthed.

"Call that young man up and let him know we'll be over this afternoon," Mr. Jones directed.

Casey

Nervous energy flowed through Casey's body. Bailey called him earlier that morning to tell him that she would be coming by to return the necklace. He wasn't pleased that she wanted to return the gift, but he committed to using the opportunity to appeal to her. He didn't know if she would come inside his house or not, so he straightened up the living room and kitchen. If he could get her past the threshold of the front door, he would offer her a beverage.

Casey hadn't worked this hard for a woman's time and attention ever and here he was going the extra mile for a woman that didn't want to date him because of a work conflict. His mother's words swirled in the back of his head, but he kept pressing forward. Regardless of her situation with Mike, Casey knew this was his last opportunity to make an impression on Bailey.

****

Casey sat on the short stoop at his front door adjacent to the driveway waiting for Bailey to arrive. She sent him a text twenty minutes earlier informing him that she was on her way along with her father and brother. Shortly after settling down Casey seen Bailey's bright red vehicle approach his circular driveway. He rose to his feet to meet the vehicle at the top of the driveway.

Seeing Bailey in the passenger seat of the car, Casey was unsure if he should wait for her to exit the car or if he should approach the vehicle. When the car finally stopped Casey elected to go the southern route and introduce himself to Bailey's family. Casey approached the driver's side of the door and gave a shy wave to her father as he waited for him to roll down the window so he could shake his hand.

"Who do we have here," an animated voice called out from the opposite side of the vehicle disrupting Casey's focus from Bailey's father.

"Hey man," Casey called out to who he assumed was Bailey's brother.

When Casey turned his attention back to Bailey's father, he found that he was exiting the vehicle and took a step back to allow the older gentleman space to comfortably exit the sports car. Holding out his right-hand

Casey proceeded to formally greet Bailey's father "Hi, Mr. Jones."

Bailey's father returned the handshake, "Hi Casey. How are you son?"

"I'm well and yourself? Are you enjoying San Diego," he asked?

"I'm Bryce," the lively voice announced approaching Mr. Jones' side.

Taking the man's hand, "Casey," he replied.

"So, you are the one giving my sister expensive gifts?" Bryce declared.

"That's enough," Bailey chastised her brother as she rounded the vehicle to stand between her flamboyant brother and co-worker, holding the black gift bag that Casey had given her last week during her birthday party. "Hi Casey," she started, "forgive my brother Bryce, he's only kidding".

"I'm not," Bryce huffed.

"You are" Bailey affirmed while rolling her eyes at her brother, "…and you have met my father", she redirected the conversation.

"Would you guys like to come in for a bit," Casey asked.

"Yes!"

"No."

Bailey and Bryce said in unison, providing conflicting answers.

Mr. Jones closely watched the interaction between Bailey and Casey, not saying a word. Casey felt like he was being judged, and he could only imagine the things Bailey had shared with her father about him. He took a deep breath to settle his rising anxiety. "You drove all the way to Chula Vista, the least you can do is stay for a minute," he argued.

For once Bryce was silent; Bailey turned to her father, "Dad, what would you like to do?" she asked the patriarch of her family.

Mr. Jones searched Casey's face as if the answer was behind his eyes. Casey felt so vulnerable and exposed. No one had looked at him in such a way since his father. Feeling satisfied with his silent inquiry Mr. Jones answered his daughter while not breaking eye contact with Casey, "Let's go in for a while."

"Right this way," Casey led the family up the walkway toward his home. Behind his back he could hear Bailey's audible displeasure with the decision her father made while Bryce commented on everything that was on the path leading up to the front door.

Bailey

"Can I get you all anything to drink," Casey asked.

"I'll take a beer if you have one," Mr. Jones answered first.

"Water is fine for me," Bailey replied.

"A dirty martini for me" Bryce requested. Bailey shot her brother a menacing glare which demanded he change his beverage request immediately.

"Water will be fine," Bryce amended.

The Jones' found their way inside of Casey's modest living room and sought a seat on his oversized sectional couch. "Dad, why would you agree to come inside this man's house?" Bailey asked hastily after Casey left for the kitchen to grab their beverages.

"Curiosity," he replied not offering further detail.

"Curiosity, really?" Bailey chastised. "We were supposed to come here for a simple drop off, and now we're inside his home."

"Who doesn't want to see how the rich and famous live," Bryce interjected.

"Fine," Bailey conceded, "you guys can have ten minutes of fun, but then we need to go."

Casey returned to the living room with a serving tray filled with a beer, three bottles of water and a bowl of shelled pistachios. "I didn't know what you all liked, so I hope the pistachios work," Casey shared as he placed the serving tray onto the large ottoman which doubles as a coffee table.

"The pistachios are fine," Mr. Jones reassured.

"Good stuff" Casey replied confidently.

The four sat in an awkward silence in Casey's living room avoiding eye contact or any attempt at conversation. Bailey was experiencing a range of emotions and felt paralyzed about what she should do next. Garnering courage, Bailey broke through the silence. Reaching for the gift bag that sat next to her, Bailey handed Bryce the bag to pass along to Casey, "It is lovely, but as you already know, I can't keep it," she announced, feigning confidence.

Casey stared back at Bailey in anguish, "Okay," was all he could manage as he received the bag from Bryce.

"All right, dad, Bryce, let's go," Bailey instructed.

"You guys don't have to go so soon. Stay a while," Casey encouraged.

"Bailey," Mr. Jones spoke, "you came for what you wanted to do, now take a seat", he ordered.

"But dad…" she whined.

"But dad nothing," Mr. Jones started, "this young man invited us into his home to visit and since this is my weekend getaway I want to stay awhile and get to know Mr. Casey Christopher better."

Bailey took her seat as instructed by her father and proceeded to pull out her phone. Though her father was making her stay she didn't have to engage with anyone, so she scrolled social media and played games on her phone to keep herself entertained until the grueling visit ended.

Casey

The afternoon turned out far better than Casey imagined. Despite Bailey returning the gift he gave her; he ended up having a great time with her father and brother. Though Bryce was extremely flamboyant, he found that he was a fun person to be around who took advantage of each moment to bring life and color to any space he occupies. Mr. Jones was Casey's favorite. He was very wise and nurturing.

Sitting with Mr. Jones made Casey realize how much he missed his own father. He decided in that time, while Mr. Jones was there, he would absorb all the wisdom he could from him. Bailey started to relax a bit too, though she did not say much she did put her phone down eventually to join the conversation. It pained Casey to see how uncomfortable Bailey was in his home and in his presence with her family. In the moments they shared together he never seen her uncomfortable.

Casey considered briefly changing his seat so that he could sit next to Bailey to provide her comfort and reassurance. He, however, was no fool. Casey was well aware that any displays of affection would immediately ruin the moment and end the Jones' visit. So, he did what he could; he watched Bailey, providing reassurance with his eyes as much as possible.

Casey hadn't expected them to stay as long as they did and was pleased when they agreed to stay for an early dinner. They quickly settled on ordering Chinese food for delivery. When the food arrived, the party moved from the living room to the dining room. Casey grabbed serving utensils from their holding canister next to the stove, then followed up by grabbing plates from the cabinet. Casey was surprised to see Bryce in his refrigerator grabbing fresh beverages for everyone. Casey noted Bryce's comfort and familiarity despite being a first-time visitor.

Walking back to the dining room table, Mr. Jones and Bailey worked in silence as they took the food out of the bags, placing the cartoons in the center of the rectangular table, a warm feeling of comfort swept over Casey. For the first time since he'd lived San Diego he felt at home.

"This feels great," Casey admitted, "Next time you guys are in town let me know and I will fire up the grill."

"Absolutely! Before I leave town, I'll get your number from Bailey," Mr. Jones replied excitedly. "I know there are extenuating circumstances blocking you and Bailey from dating, but it doesn't mean we can't hang out."

"Dad! Really?" Bailey complained.

"The only way Bailey and Casey could be together is if Casey got traded," Bryce offered laughing.

"Well," Casey started, "don't tempt me because I will get my agent on the line," he joined in on the laughter.

"You can leave the Oilers all you want, brother", Bailey started. "But I still wouldn't date you. I don't do long distance relationships", Bailey concluded as she raised a bottle of water to her lips.

"Dang! She is a tough cookie" Casey exclaimed.

"Well, she did have three brothers watching over", Bryce offered. "So, baby girl knows how to hold her own in *any* situation."

"Let's stop talking about your sister as if she is not sitting here at the table with us", Mr. Jones interjected.

"Thank you, daddy," Bailey responded with gratitude.

****

Casey was still riding high when he arrived early at Oilers Stadium for their home game against the Chicago Cheetahs. The previous day with the Jones family could not have gone better. The patriarch, Mr. Jones, was a wise man who bestowed many gems for Casey to consider. And, though Bailey maintained a healthy distance between them, Casey did notice her warming up to him and his home. The best part of the evening was Bryce, Casey had never met someone so free in his life.

Growing up in a conservative home Casey and his siblings always had to do or say the right thing. Discipline and order were non-negotiable in the Christopher household. In the Jones household, the children were allowed to color outside of the lines and Casey noted how Bryce was the representative for how Bailey and her brothers were raised. It felt liberating talking to Bryce and observing how he showed up in the world.

Casey was ecstatic, though kept a cool exterior, when Mr. Jones shared that he would bring his other sons with him the next time he visited. He could not put his finger on it, but the promise made by Mr. Jones felt like acceptance into his family, like he was building a relationship with the man that was independent of the man's daughter. He still wanted her, too. Reality allowed him to accept that that was not an option.

"Earth to Casey", Jamal said as he waved his large hand in front of Casey's face to get his attention.

"W-what?" Casey replied snapping back to attention.

"Bro, what's got you in a chipper mood and arriving to the stadium early?"

Grinning like a cheshire cat, Casey dropped his head to hide his grin. "Bro? What is it?" Jamal continued to pry.

"Yesterday I spent the day with Bailey and her family", Casey admitted.

"Swear?" Jamal asked in disbelief.

"Yeah, man!"

"Shut up!" Jamal continued in disbelief.

"Yes! Bailey, her pops and her brother came over in the afternoon. She came over to return her birthday gift. At first, I was nervous because I didn't know how her father would respond to me. To my surprise he was mad cool. He reminded me of my own father. And, her brother, bro! He is a one-man comedy show."

Jamal was speechless as he listened to his friend and teammate share the details of his evening. "So, you are going to infiltrate the family to get to her?" Jamal asked.

"Actually, no. I respect Bailey and her decision. Her father is mad cool, and I could use more of his wisdom. Talking to him reminded me of my own father."

"If you say so, just be careful, bro." Jamal cautioned.

Sighing, Casey responded, "I got this, don't worry".

The men turned to their lockers as they began to dress for warmups. As the noise increased in the locker room from more players and staff arriving and milling about, Casey considered Jamal's question regarding his motivation of getting to know Bailey's family better. He really did feel a kinship with her father, and he honestly wanted to keep in touch with him. But, that question had him reeling. Casey decided to push the question aside as he began to mentally prepare to take the field.

Bailey

Bailey dreaded the day and what she planned to do by the end of it. After she and her family spent time with Casey at his Chula Vista home over the weekend something sparked within her. Something that was frightening. Something that was comforting. Something that was forbidden. She needed to work her feelings for Casey out, or rather, how she wanted to address her feelings for Casey. And, Bailey knew she would not be able to do that with Mike lingering.

It had been over a week since Bailey and Mike last spoke, they argued the morning after her birthday and Bailey was still upset that he had yet to apologize for ruining her birthday weekend. Arguments and differences aside, Bailey knew things with Mike were not working. He was a nice guy who, on the surface, checked all of the boxes, but Bailey had to be honest that she could not see a path forward with him.

****

Bailey hastily crossed the parking lot for La Puerta's entrance, she chose the Gaslamp bar and restaurant for happy hour with Michael because it was equidistance to their homes, and she loved their cocktails. Entering the restaurant through its ornate double doors, Bailey made a beeline for the bar area. She'd hoped to beat Michael, but as she scanned the bar for two seats, she found him in a corner booth. Bailey silently thanked God for Mike's astuteness of the situation. Something in Bailey told her he was aware that their situation would soon be ending.

"Hey, you," Bailey said as she approached the booth where Mike was sitting.

"Hey, yourself", Mike replied as he rose from the booth to greet Bailey with a hug.

Bailey hesitated for half a second before joining Mike in what was sure to be their last embrace. "I see you beat me here", she said matter-of-factly in an attempt to break the ice or to settle her nerves. Bailey was surprised by how nervous she was. A woman who handled multi-millionaires regularly should not be intimated by a conversation she initiated. And, yet Bailey thought to herself, here she was. "How was your day?" Bailey inquired as she broke away from Mike to sit down opposite him in the booth he secured for them.

"The day was good", he started, "nothing too exciting, just business as usual".

"That's wonderful", Bailey replied in an attempt to sound interested. Her mind was running at hyper speed, and she was trying desperately to calm her nerves.

"How was yours?"

"It was pretty mundane," Bailey answered as Mike bore into her. She suddenly became aware that Mike was assessing her. He had not taken his eyes off of her since she arrived. And the only time they did not have eye contact was when she broke it. Fidgeting with the straps of her orange Telfar bag Bailey mindlessly blurted out, "I returned the necklace. The one Casey gave me for my birthday."

Bailey had idea why she would ungracefully share the update on the necklace. She certainly planned on telling Mike, but the way it spilled out of her mouth left her in shock of herself. "Cool", was all Mike offered in response.

"I know it was an issue when we last spoke and I wanted to let you know how I followed up with it", she responded.

"Unbelievable", Mike started.

"What are you talking about?" Bailey asked, confused by his sudden change in disposition.

"I'm talking about you, Bailey!"

"The first thing out of your mouth was about that necklace as if you returning that man's gift solves everything". Bailey started to interrupt, but Mike cut her off, "the fact that he felt comfortable enough gifting you something like that is the problem. No man buys a woman jewelry if he isn't in a relationship with her or trying to be in a relationship with her." Bailey opened and shut her mouth as Mike went on, "Yes, men and women can be platonic friends. And, in these friendships there are unwritten rules that everyone knows. Buying your friend a diamond necklace," Mike gestured air quotes around the word friend, "is completely out of bounds. Are you fucking that nigga?" he asked outright.

Bailey was stunned at Mike's choice of words. He rarely swore and almost never used the n-word. He was more upset than what he was leading on to be. "I chose you", Bailey offered. After your pissing contest with Casey in the parking lot the day you surprised me at work, I chose you."

"To answer your question, no, I have never been intimate with Casey. Like I've said countless times, we work together, and I am not willing to jeopardize my career by even considering a relationship with him", Bailey reassured.

"So, if y'all didn't work together are you telling me that you would fuck with him?" Mike placed his elbows on the table and rested his chin on his fists awaiting Bailey's response.

"I don't know what point you are trying to prove here, but I am not going to entertain your hang up about my friendship with Casey. Like I said, I sensed the tension between the two of you when you were at my job and I thought you knew that I had chosen you. Clearly my efforts were in vain because you already had an alternate storyline floating in your head."

A waiter approached their table to take their drink order; Mike ordered a beer and Bailey ordered a Cadillac margarita. When the waiter was out of earshot, Bailey continued, "Look, Mike, I did not invite you here to fight and argue, nor did I invite you here to prove anything to you." Mike scoffed at her last statement but did not interrupt as he lowered his hands and slouched back in his seat. "I came here because I wanted to talk. You have not returned any of my calls nor have you tried to apologize for ruining my birthday weekend."

"Apologize? You must be out of your mind. Apologize. What a joke, wow!" Bailey was taken aback by Mike's crass tone. She was in disbelief that the man she'd been dating could be so stubborn and cold towards her. Bailey had hoped by the time their meeting ended they could agree to be friends, mainly due to Sierra and Corey. They shared friends and would have to be amicable with one another for their friends' sake.

"I didn't realize you needed more time to process how the last two weeks had been. I figured enough time had passed and we could talk things out." Bailey ignored Mike's obnoxious grunt. "I have had a great time dating you and getting to know you over these last few months. And, while I was hoping we would eventually enter an exclusive relationship, I now see that that is not possible. You are a great guy..."

"I know that", Mike interrupted.

"But I don't think it is going to work between us. It is unfortunate that we are not able to resolve our differences and find a path forward, but hey. I wish you understood that I cannot control what other people do and that you could trust me enough to know when people attempt to get out of bounds with me that I correct them. That is not the case, so here we are." Bailey paused as the waiter returned with beverages. Grabbing her margarita as soon as the waiter placed in on the coaster in front of her, Bailey took a massive sip of the tangy yet sweet cocktail.

"For the sake of Sierra and Corey I do hope that we can be friends one day. I know it will be awkward at first, but I do believe we can be cordial with one another."

"I see you have it all figured out," Mike chastised as he took a sip of his beer. "Why lead with the necklace when you knew coming here you were going to end things?" Mike asked. "Why even invite me out if you already had your mind made up about what you wanted to do, Bailey?" Bailey made no attempt to offer Mike a response, instead she watched him drink his beer as he attempted to maintain his composure.

"I think you are right", Mike admitted to Bailey's surprise. "We have different perspectives and expectations and the two will probably never be reconciled. Before we take this any further, we do need to call it quits. Corey is my boy and Sierra is your girl which means we will have to see each other off the strength of them." Bailey was pleased to hear Mike come around to her side and agree on no longer dating. "But…", he continued, "I am going to need a minute. I felt like we would be having this conversation, I just didn't want it to be true. I was hoping you would understand how I felt as a man about recent events and that's just not possible."

"To be honest, Mike, I do understand how you feel. I just needed you to trust me. But more than that, I needed you to own how your behavior impacted my birthday weekend. I have shared with you on many occasions about how important birthdays and holidays are to me in my life."

"Yeah, well, here we are."

"So, I've actually never done anything like this. What do we do now?" Bailey asked.

"Lady, you are a certified mess! I am trying to be mad at you for breaking my heart and dumping me and you over there with jokes", Mike kidded.

"Mike, seriously, thank you. Thank you for everything and for making this part of the process easy, even though you started out being a jerk a little bit."

"Jerk?" Mike asked feigning hurt by her words. "You dump a brotha publicly and think it's going to be glitter and rainbows? Ya'll women are a trip."

"Don't say that", Bailey pleaded, "I did not dump you. You know just as well as I do, that we needed to end our courtship."

"I mean, I felt like things had been off for a minute but figured it would pass. But it doesn't mean you still didn't break my heart."

"Lord!" Bailey interrupted in feigned frustration.

"So, since you broke my heart and I am slowly dying inside you, my dear, are going to buy me dinner and I am going to order the most expensive thing on the menu."

"Sure" Bailey responded bemused, "if that's what it takes to course correct and start our friendship anew, then so be it."

Once the hard part of the conversation was over, Mike and Bailey enjoyed a nice dinner and platonic conversation. Bailey was hopeful that the two of them could grow to become good friends, for now, she would not push and allow him to define the dynamics of their newly redefined friendship. As the evening wound down and the waiter brought the check, always the consummate gentleman, Mike paid despite telling Bailey she owed him dinner. She tried to argue and insisted this go-round would be on her. Mike obliged that request, though he had no intentions on ever having Bailey or anyone woman pay his way.

Casey

The gym always served as a good distraction for Casey. Whether he was excited or angry, Casey used the gym to release the energy flowing through his body to maintain his sanity, or rather, to be able to think rationally. This morning, Casey was punishing his body to release the anxiety flowing through his veins. He received a message from Bailey the night before asking to meet for happy hour, and since then Casey's mind had been reeling. The woman evoked so much emotion from him.

After his workout Casey went through his regular mid-week routine of treatment with the athletic trainers, position meeting with the defensive line coach and a meeting with the defensive coordinator to go over the strategy for their upcoming game. Once all of his obligations for the day were completed and he was barely functional, he went home for a midday nap.

****

Casey cursed himself as he impatiently waited for the light to change colors across the street from the Edgewater Grill, the restaurant where he was set to meet Bailey. Being late was not a big issue for Casey, however, he felt guilty being late meeting her for happy hour. He clonked out on his couch when he arrived home from his workouts and team meetings. He'd planned to nap for an hour before getting ready for his evening plans, with the intention of arriving at Edgewater ahead of Bailey.

Casey woke up nearly three hours later and was in desperate need of a shower, so skipping one to save time was not an option. Taking a shower would add an additional thirty minutes to his tardiness. As he quickly showered and dressed Casey contemplated his options for apologizing to Bailey for his negligence and tardiness. Knowing his gesture could not be lavish or expensive, when Casey got in his car, he decided to call the restaurant for a Hail Mary favor.

He pulled up furiously to the valet and exchanged his key for a ticket hurriedly walking to the restaurant's entrance. Placing a hand on the door, Casey took a brief moment to brace himself and prepare for a meeting he desperately wanted and felt unprepared for. Scanning the bar area of the restaurant, Casey located Bailey sitting at the bar engaging in a conversation with one of the bartenders. If he wasn't running late Casey would have been upset that Bailey was laughing and smiling at another man when those should be reserved for him – since she was there to meet him. Under the current circumstances, Casey was pleased that she was not sitting alone bored or upset.

"Hey stranger", Casey said as he slid on the stool next to Bailey.

"Don't 'hey stranger' me", she responded.

"Well, you would probably lecture me if I called you beautiful, so 'stranger' will have to suffice for now".

"Anyways", Bailey interrupted with a feigned sense of annoyance, "what were you doing that had you almost an hour late?"

"I'm not even gonna BS you", Casey started, "I was sleep".

"Seriously?"

"Seriously", he reassured her. "I see the manager relayed the message that I was going to be late", Casey confirmed as he pulled one of the yellow roses from the vase that sat between them.

"Indeed, he did. They are beautiful, by the way. Thank you."

On his drive to the restaurant from his home, Casey called the restaurant and asked the General Manager to inform Bailey he would be late and to do something – anything to demonstrate how apologetic he was for such a misstep. Much to Casey's surprise, the two dozen yellow roses were perfect, and he could not be more grateful to Dan for coming through in the clutch like that.

"So, how was your day?" Casey asked in an attempt to avoid the uncomfortable silence.

"The day was good. Nothing too exciting happened."

"Is that a good thing or bad?" Casey quizzed.

"Great question!" Bailey started. "I suppose I don't want to label it good or bad. It just was. Does that make sense?"

"I gotchu!"

Bailey fell silent and diverted her gaze from Casey. He wondered what she was thinking about, what suddenly distracted her from conversing with him. Casey was curious, and he didn't want to pry so he waited until she rejoined him.

"Thank you for being so nice to my dad and brother the other weekend."

"It was no problem," Casey shared.

"I know you had a game, and we stayed later than anticipated."

"You didn't anticipate staying at all."

"True, but that's not the point. You were kind to them, and I truly appreciate your generosity and hospitality."

"Your pops is a cool guy and that Bryce is a character", Casey suddenly fell silent, unsure of how much he should divulge to Bailey. "For real, though, I loved having you and your family over. Your dad reminds me of my old man, and it was nice to be laced with game. I don't have that anymore, so it felt nice to have an older man look out for me. You're really lucky to have him."

Chewing on her bottom lip, Bailey tried to choose her words carefully. "Your father died?" She asked. "Did I know this?"

"Yeah, he died my senior year of college, right before I got drafted." Casey started drumming his fingers on the bar top to create a calming rhythmic sound. "He never got a chance to watch me play pro," he concluded.

"Thank you for sharing," Bailey started. "To think I've had a crush on you for years and didn't realize your dad passed".

"Yeah well, I don't really talk… Wait a minute! You have a crush on me?"

"Had," Bailey clarified.

Shifting in her seat, Bailey made an attempt to redirect the conversation back to the original topic. "My dad likes you, too. Dare I say he was impressed by your hospitality and humanity."

"That's what's up."

"I know you invited him and all my brothers back for a bar-b-que, but I want to let you know that you do not have to do that. I appreciate the sentiment but in no way do I want you to feel obligated in hosting them."

"Did you not just hear me say how much I like your father?" Casey began to chastise her, "He and your brothers have an open invitation to visit whenever they are in town.

I'd understand if you wouldn't want to come, but I enjoy and need genuine people around me. Between my mother and your brother, Bryce, they keep me humble, and I appreciate that."

"Interesting, but okay."

"What's that supposed to mean?" Casey asked.

"It doesn't mean anything. I was aware you exchanged numbers with my dad, I just wasn't sure to what extent you were expecting to keep in touch with him."

"Look, Bailey, I know you have your thoughts about me because I am professional athlete, but football is my occupation it does not define me. Underneath the helmet and shoulder pads I am a regular person who desire the same things as everyone else."

"Fair enough. We should probably order."

Bailey

Bailey had been so consumed with her conversation with Casey that she didn't realize the bartender had not come over to take their order or that the bar area was completely empty. It was mid-evening so patrons should still be milling about the restaurant. But that wasn't the case, at least for the bar area. The customers who were in the bar area when she arrived had since departed. She suspected Casey had something to do with the bar area being closed just to them. She prayed silently that the man across from her didn't have the entire restaurant closed to the public.

She couldn't ponder her environment further because Casey called the bartender over to take their meal and drink order. Bailey ordered steak nachos and her usual Cadillac margarita. Casey kept it simple and ordered grilled chicken and rice with a tequila straight up.

"Did you have the restaurant shutdown?" she asked, the words spontaneously spilling out of her mouth.

Casey chuckled as he shook his head, "Is that a problem?" He answered.

"It seems a bit excessive to me," Bailey answered.

"I was late, and I was nervous about what you wanted to talk about so I asked the General Manager if he could close the bar for me until we left," he answered honestly.

"I see. And what were you so nervous about?"

"You!" Casey responded emphatically.

"What do you mean me?"

"I mean, you sent a cryptic message about wanting to talk and do happy hour when the last time we spoke, you basically told me to fuck off."

"Now you're just being dramatic, I did not tell you to fuck off."

"You didn't say those words exactly, but that was definitely the energy you carried."

"Interesting," Bailey started, "well, that was not my intention. I needed you to understand and respect my position."

"And I do, loud and clear."

"Good!"

"So, why did you ask me out on date?"

Pushing Casey in his left bicep, Bailey responded, "Not a date."

"Sure."

"Anyways," Bailey started as she rolled her eyes. "I have a problem that I want to run by you and get your opinion on."

"Say what now?" Casey joked as he sat up in his seat, "the great Bailey Jones wants my opinion? Little old me, Casey of the San Diego Oilers?"

"You are so silly," she chuckled, "can you be serious for one second, please."

"Yes, give me one second" Casey said as he made multiple failed attempts at straightening his face from traces of laughter. "I'm ready", he said as he rolled his lips inward.

Bailey sat tall in her seat as she gathered the courage to make one of the greatest admissions she had ever made in life. "Long story short, I ended things with a guy who I thought I could be with because he was safe and comfortable." Casey repositioned himself so that he was no longer leaning on the bar and staring straight at Bailey. "But that's not the issue I'm trying to sort out. I'm trying to reconcile in my mind how the forbidden guy that I like feels like the sweetest thing I've ever known. Do you know what I mean?" Casey offered a head nod in response.

"This isn't about what I let go of because there wasn't much there. I feel like I'm fighting myself, trying to convince myself to leave the forbidden fruit alone because I am afraid that it will be rotten. And, if the forbidden fruit is rotten, then it can potentially spoil everything, and I cannot afford that type of disruption in my life."

Bailey watched as Casey rose from his seat after she completed her monologue. Unsure what he was preparing to do, she kept her eyes locked with his and waited. She did not have to wait too long because Casey grabbed Bailey hands from the bar and pulled her up to stand facing him. Never breaking eye contact, Bailey searched Casey's eyes for reassurance and Casey searched her eyes for permission. When he found the answer to his question Casey wrapped Bailey inside his muscular frame for an embrace. He squeezed her gently to let her know he was there with her, that he was there for her and that he understood.

Slowly Casey could feel Bailey's body relax inside his arms causing his heart to skip with excitement. He held on longer because he did not want to let her go, she felt like home in his arms. Casey didn't know what would happen in the future or next, so he wanted to savor every precious moment of their sweet embrace. Leaning down, Casey kissed her forehead, then he leaned in further towards her left ear and said, "I'm here with you and we will figure this out together."

About the Author

Ziggy Harris is a passionate romance novelist whose pen weaves tales of resilience, love, and empowerment. Hailing from the vibrant city of San Francisco, California, Ziggy draws inspiration from her rich heritage and personal experiences to craft stories that resonate deeply with readers.

She brings to life characters who defy stereotypes and overcome adversity with grace and strength. Ziggy celebrates the beauty of diversity and the power of representation by creating characters that resonate with readers, capturing the essence and complexities of human relationships, love and life transitions.

With a growing collection of acclaimed novels, including "Not In His Shadow" Ziggy Harris continues to captivate audiences with her powerful storytelling and unwavering commitment to authenticity.

When she's not lost in the world of her imagination, Ziggy can be found enjoying live music, traveling, or attending live sporting events.

www.ingramcontent.com/pod-product-compliance
Lightning Source LLC
Chambersburg PA
CBHW030804210726
48290CB00002B/411